A WORLD OF OTHERS
A FANTASY

by

Aaron Wickstrom and Sandor Czekus

The contents of this work, including, but not limited to, the accuracy of events, people, and places depicted; opinions expressed; permission to use previously published materials included; and any advice given or actions advocated are solely the responsibility of the author, who assumes all liability for said work and indemnifies the publisher against any claims stemming from publication of the work.

Dorrance Publishing Co
585 Alpha Drive
Pittsburgh, PA 15238
Visit our website at *www.dorrancebookstore.com*

ISBN: 978-1-6853-7342-9
eISBN: 978-1-6853-7658-1

CONTENTS

1. THE GIFT 1

2. THE UNDEAD 23

3. RESCUE..47

4. THE GODDESS OF RAMPAGE 71

THE GIFT

Once upon a time, in a land of beautiful crystal-clear waters and hills that bloomed with wild flowers of every color and mountains that reached to the heavens filled with creatures big and small, there was a very old wizard who lived in a shack by some beautiful and peaceful water falls.

One day, something strange occurred. There was a little fairy who appeared and asked him for help to defeat the darkness that was coming; a time of pure evil that would destroy this universe was approaching.

The wizard said, "I'm old and frail, but I'll do what I can."

He picked up his magical staff and the two of them started walking down the path. It was the beginning of a new adventure.

When they stopped to rest their weary bones, he began to speak to his new friend.

"I have seen many things in my time. I have seen newborn suns, dying stars, and far-out worlds beyond belief, with a beauty that others can only imagine; black holes like bottomless pits that seems to go on forever; forests with vines that twist and tangle without end... For many years, I have traveled this world and many others, searching for enlightenment that has always been just out of my grasp. As I sit here, I grow tired, and my time is short." He told his friend, "I'm afraid I won't make it to the end."

As the glow faded from his eyes, he spoke his final words. The fairy heard him say softly, "I'm sorry."

As she felt a warm welcoming grow about her, the wizard had given her one last gift: all his power as he drifted from this old world to the next. She had never received such a gift, and she was moved.

After a few moments, she wiped the tears from her eyes, gathered everything together and started on her way down the path. After a short time, she decided to rest by a large stone. As the birds were singing and the flowers bloomed in the morning dew, she listened to the beautiful sounds as she ate her meal. Small animals came out from their hiding places, so she shared her meager meal with them.

Suddenly, the forest became quiet, and she heard a small child's cry off in the distance. She arose and started towards the distressed cry. As she slowly approached the small child, she noticed something odd laying near to the small child. It was her father. He was severely hurt with an orc arrow stuck in his right side. As she walked over to him and carefully removed the orc's arrow and placed her hand gently over the wound. She felt a warm glow as he began to heal.

A short while later, he sat up and embraced his beautiful daughter. He told the fairy, "Thank you," as tears rolled down the side of his face. When the sobbing stopped, he asked, "Young lady, who are you?"

"My name is Mayflower. I'm on a quest to a faraway land."

He said, "I'm not a wealthy man, but I would like to show you my appreciation for helping me. Can I offer you a hot meal and a place for you to rest for the night?"

She replied, "Thank you, I accept your most generous offer." And they traveled together to his home.

Soon, she sat by a warm fire, eating a cooked meal. As night fell and the embers died, the night became cool. She stayed comfortable in her soft, warm bed and had pleasant dreams throughout the night.

She awoke feeling rested and refreshed, ready to continue her quest. She wanted to say thank you for the old man's kindness, so she pulled a blue and a green gem from her belt pouch and placed them under the pillow to be found later.

She stepped, out and once again started down the path. She traveled all day, and as the sun was setting, she came upon a fork in the road. One path went through the city; the other went through the crystal forest. She decided to follow the path through the forest. As night began to fall, she thought it would be good to stop for the night. After making camp and having a meal, she slowly started to drift into slumber.

The next morning, she awoke to a loud roar. She was filled with fear and ran to hide. When she saw a strange dwarf with green hair wearing a frying pan on his head like a helmet, it looked like the strange dwarf was in a fight with a huge brown bear over meat being cooked on a stick. As she watched, the huge bear stood up and swung his massive arm, hitting the strange dwarf across the chest and ripping open a wide gash. As blood poured out onto the ground, he let out a loud grunt.

Mayflower was horrified by the scene in front of her. The strange dwarf spoke saying, "Me, me, bear!" as he swung his war hammer with one hand, hitting the huge bear in the right knee, bringing the massive beast to the ground. He swung his frying pan with his other hand, hitting the animal across the face; then with his war hammer, he took one final blow with all his might, yelling, "Me, me, brother, die, die, beast!" and crushed the skull of the huge bear. He fell to the ground, holding his bloody chest and gasping for air then passed out.

Mayflower came out of her hiding place with a look of terror on her face. She couldn't believe what just happened. She felt that she had to help this strange dwarf somehow. She saw his bloody wound and knew that she could heal him. She gently placed her hand over his wound, closed her eyes, and felt the power flow through her as he began to heal.

He slowly opened his eyes and said, "You, you, me, help?"

She giggled and answered, "Yes, I helped you. What is your name?"

"Me, me, Dwindle."

She replied, "I'm Mayflower, pleased to meet you, Dwindle."

He said, "Me, me, food, hungry you?" as he pointed to the meat on a stick.

They sat and shared the meal. Before she knew it, it became late, and he fell fast asleep, so she cleaned up and laid down to rest herself. She found it was hard to sleep with his rumbling snores.

The next morning, to her surprise, she awoke to find a breakfast already prepared for her. As they finished their meal, she asked, "Which way are you heading?" He simply pointed down the path in the direction she was heading. She said, "I'm going that way, too. If you would like to join me, you may." He nodded his head and forgot he was drinking at the time, which made a mess and made her laugh.

They started down the path together. In a short time, her strange friend became excited and took off running to a large tree that had another dwarf hanging upside down by a vine. A short kobold was poking at him with a spear. Dwindle took his war hammer and, in one mighty blow, took out the short kobold. He was jumping up and down, saying, "Me, me, brother."

Mayflower cut the other dwarf down as he grumbled about getting caught in a simple, stupid trap. When he was free, Mayflower could see that these two were twins. The second dwarf stood up, brushed himself off, and said:

"Thank you. My name is Kindle; I see that you've already met my brother Dwindle."

As this was going on, in another area of the forest, a fierce battle was taking place. A large barbarian was fighting over a dozen orcs. Up in a tree hiding on a thick branch was an elf archer, watching in total amazement at his ability to fight all these orcs. As the barbarian lay waste to one orc after the next, he turned, swinging his mighty sword and burying it deep within another orc's chest. He caught a bow to his chest, causing flesh to tear and a very deep slash in his upper right leg, which made him stumble for a moment. He seemed more determined than ever as the battle raged on. He stabbed one orc, turned, and sliced another in two. With great speed, he plunged his sword to the hilt, stabbing two orcs at the same time. He used his foot to kick the dead bodies from his bloody blade.

As warm liquid poured onto the battlefield, it looked as though victory was at hand when all of a sudden, his feet came out from under him. He slipped and hit his head on a bloody rock, knocking himself out.

A short time later, he opened his eyes and noticed that he was leaning against a blood-covered boulder and bound in chins with two orcs standing guard while the remaining orcs sat around a camp fire several yards away cooking human body parts. He inspected his open battle wounds.

Not a sound was made as the guards fell to the ground having been shot with precise accuracy, killing them with one arrow each. As the barbarian looked up in surprise, an elf leaped down from the tree holding a long knife and landing in front of two orcs, surprising them and stabbing the first one right in the neck as blood sprayed out to cover her. Before the other orc could react, with great speed, she sliced him across the belly, spilling his guts as he fell to the ground dead. Silently, she made her way to the barbarian and began to set him free.

Once free, the barbarian spotted his sword covered in orc blood lying by a tree. He ran to his weapon as an orc emerged from a bush with his arms loaded with human body parts. The orc had a look of surprise on his face as the barbarian swung his great sword and removed its head, and its body fell to the ground. The barbarian turned and charged with a furious look on his face as the remaining orcs scrambled to recover their weapons.

Six orcs never stood a chance as they dropped with arrows sticking out if them. The barbarian slashed his way through the rest. In a short time, he looked around and realized he was the last one standing with body parts littering the ground. He sat to rest with orc blood mixed with his own blood dripping from his battle wounds onto the ground.

As the elf slowly approached him, a small, furry creature crossed her path, dragging a belt pouch up to the barbarian. It dropped the pouch and jumped into his arms. The elf approached cautiously, saying, "Your friend?" in the ancient elfin language. It had been years since the barbarian heard this language, and it took some time to reply.

"I'm Lark of the Northern tribe, and this is my friend Little Thief. Who are you?"

The elf replied, "My name is Amber of the mystic forest. I observed your battle. You are truly a great warrior."

He said, "And you are a deadly archer. Would you like to join me?"

She sat with him and saw that his wounds were deep and offered to tend to them. She said, "Bring me water, so I can clean your wounds."

He stood, and that's when she first noticed how big and muscular he was. When he returned, she got busy cleaning and bandaging while Little Thief kept getting in the way. Lark scooped his little friend up and placed him in the pouch, so she could finish what she had started.

They shared a meal. As they sat talking, they heard a voice in the distance saying, "Me, me, brother," as Amber fled into the safety of the trees.

Mayflower and the dwarf twins found their way through the dense forest. They came upon the battlefield, where they could see a fierce battle had just taken place. Mayflower looked around and saw a large barbarian sitting alone. Mayflower and the brothers slowly started to approach the wounded barbarian. At that moment, two arrows struck the ground at their feet. He said, "The second shot is to show you that the first was no mistake." Then he said, "Watch."

As he flipped a gold coin into the air, it was struck by another arrow.

Mayflower said, "We mean no harm. My name is Mayflower, and these dwarfs are Dwindle and Kindle. We are on a quest to the great valley. We are tired from our day's travel, may we join you and rest?"

The barbarian nodded and said, "My name is Lark and my friend in the trees, her name is Amber." He went to get Little Thief from his belt pouch, but he was nowhere to be found. After a little while, Amber came down from the trees and silently approached the group. The barbarian spoke in a language Mayflower and the dwarfs did not understand. Amber sat next to Lark as Lark explained to the group, "Amber only speaks her ancient elfin tongue."

About that time, Dwindle jumped up, and pulling the pan from his head, he said, "Me, me, food," and started chasing a small ferret that was dragging a small belt pouch toward his friend. Lark jumped up with surprising speed, which stopped Dwindle dead in his tracks.

As his brother felt a sharp blade against his throat, Kindle was surprised to find Amber prepared to help this barbarian. Lark spoke, saying, "He is my friend. His name is Little Thief. He brings me gifts; he does this often."

Dwindle said, "Me, me, food."

Lark said, "No! He is my friend."

Kindle spoke up, saying, "That's my belt pouch that little thing stole."

Lark tossed the pouch back to Kindle.

Mayflower said, "You have been hurt, may I help you with your wounds?"

"No!" he said, "I do not like magic."

She said, "Very well then."

After a while, the brothers and the Barbarian fell asleep. Mayflower sat up, covering her ears thinking, she'd get no rest with all three snoring, one louder than the next. As she looked over and saw Amber sleep peacefully and Little Thief curled next to her in a ball, she wondered how in the world she was going to get any rest. She closed her eyes and whispered a magic spell to take away her hearing until sun rise, and she was able to sleep soundly.

The next morning, they awoke to find a good meal for them to enjoy.

Mayflower said, "I hope you enjoy this hot meal."

Lark said, "Thank you," as he grabbed a large bowl of food and began to eat. Lark noticed Dwindle and Kindle licking their bowls clean after they ate. Lark sat to clean and care for his blade.

As Little Thief scurried about, Dwindle was watching his every move, whispering, "Yum!" over and over again. Lark jumped to his feet, scooping up his little friend and placing him safely in his belt pouch. He gave Dwindle a sharp glare, and tightening his grip on his sword, he said, "No!"

Amber noticed what was going on and grinned to herself as she thought, *This dwarf doesn't stand a chance against my man.*

As they prepared for the day's journey, Amber spoke something only Lark could understand, and Lark pointed a finger at Dwindle and laughed. At the same time, Dwindle pointed a finger at Lark and laughed as well. Kindle approached the couple and asked, "Which way are you two going?"

Lark answered, "Where I go, she goes."

Mayflower was puzzled by his answer and asked, "Will you join our quest?"

Lark answered, "Where she goes, I go."

Dwindle ran to Lark, grabbing his massive arm and began to tug, saying, "Come, come, fun, fun."

Mayflower spoke and explained about their quest.

Lark replied, "Your quest is noble. My blade is at your service."

After a short time of arrival, they encountered someone cloaked in robe's sitting on the path with a wooden sword staked into the ground. Dwindle ran to the sword to free it from its place, yelling words that no-one could understand. In a flash, Dwindle went flying backwards as this person stood, having hit Dwindle with one blow. Dwindle had one foot print across his chest.

Kindle rushed forward to help his brother and was knocked to the ground as well. When he had gotten up, he had a palm print imprinted on his chest. The stranger pulled back her hood to reveal a beautiful young woman.

Lark said, "I should have known it was you. No one moves that fast. I thought you were dead."

She said, "Your group is so loud, you'll never sneak up on anyone. I am on my way home to rest. Prepare your selves for tonight. A storm is on its way." Then she continued on her journey.

Little Thief scurried on the ground, and Dwindle took off after him, saying, "Me, me, food, yum!"

Kindle said, "Oh no, here we go again."

Lark tripped him, saying, "No, no!" as Dwindle fell on his face in the mud.

Kindle jumped in front of Lark, saying, "If you want to pick on my brother, you'll have to deal with me, and we'll see how long you will last."

Lark said, "Keep your brother away from Little Thief, and we will have no problems."

Dwindle stood covered in mud. Mayflower approached him to help. She cast a spell, and the filth vanished.

When they reached the edge of the forest, the path split into three directions. They stopped, trying to figure out which way to proceed. Mayflower reached into her belt pouch and pulled out a small red stone and as she tossed it in the air, she whispered show me. The red stone landed a short distance away, letting them know which path to take. There was a blur on the path, Little Thief grabbed at his prize and was turned to stone. Mayflower said, my magical items are protected as she cast a spell to return Little Thief back to normal. Lark watched this happen with anger building deep inside of him.

As they started down the path they came upon a cliff. There was a rope bridge spanning across a thousand-foot crevice. Kindle in front, Dwindle behind, the pair started swinging the rope bridge. As they were laughing, Mayflower yelled, "Stop that, you two."

Dwindle said, "Me, me, brother, weeee!"

The swinging continued as Amber ran across the swinging bridge laughing. Lark gripped the sides with all his might, afraid of plunging to his death. In a short while, the brothers tired of their little game, and finally, they made it across. Amber thought it was so funny that this big strong man was afraid of something so silly. She told Lark, "No harm done; they were just having fun!"

By noon, they came to a ledge. Looking over, they saw a great field of large boulders with a path that twisted and turned, disappearing into the distance. Mayflower thought she saw some movement just beyond some large boulders as they slowly made their way down to the path.

Suddenly, Dwindle slipped and began to tumble, taking out Lark as they both tumble to the bottom. When the group caught up, they pulled Lark off of Dwindle. He was gasping for breath under the big man. When they both stood up Lark said, "You stupid oaf! You did that on purpose."

Dwindle replied, "You, you, clumsy brute."

Mayflower saw that Little Thief got injured in the tumble, so she healed him, which made Lark furious.

Amber told him, "There's no reason to be angry. No magic was on you."

Then she ran up the hill and retrieved Dwindle's frying pan and placed it on his head as she smiled.

Lark said, "Stupid little man."

Mayflower said, "Let's keep going. We still have a long way to travel."

A short time later, they stopped for a rest. Mayflower started to prepare a meal as Kindle disappeared to relieve himself. He stood in front of a large boulder that started to move. An eye opened up to watch him. The boulder started to transform. A large creature made of rock stood before him and spoke, saying, "How dare you do that on me!"

The others gathered around to see what was going on. A little furry blue raced past with Dwindle in pursuit, saying, "Me, me, food, yum, yum!" and he ran straight into the rock creature and bounced backwards.

The creature looked down and said, "I've never seen anyone like this before."

Lark asked, "What kind of creature are you?"

"I'm Grouk of the rock giants. I stay here and give warning to all who pass. Beware, danger lies beyond the forest. Many perils lay in wait for all travelers."

Mayflower asked Grauk, "What dangers can we expect?" Without an answer, Grauk transformed back into the large boulder he once was. Mayflower stamped her feet saying, "How rude!"

They all went back and filled their bellies with a good meal that Mayflower prepared. As they sat to enjoy their meal, Mayflower asked Lark, "Why do you get mad and fight so much?"

He answered, "I seek battle. I wish to kill as many orcs as there are gods in the sky, so I will always be remembered as a great warrior."

As they finished talking, the sun began to set, and they decided to make camp for the night.

While looking for a shallow cave to shelter in, a stranger approached, asking, "May I join you and warm myself by your campfire?"

Before anyone could answer, four more strangers jumped out, and faster than your eyes could see, Amber shot two with her bow. Kindle rushed in with his war hammer as one of the strangers pulled out a short sword in one hand and a long knife with the other and was able to deliver a very deep gash across Kindle's face. Dwindle rushed in to help his brother, taking his frying pan from his head swinging it like a club. Mayflower was standing by a large boulder. As her eyes began to glow blue, she cast a spell of armor on the brothers. The brothers were surprised as the armor appeared on them.

Lark stepped forward with his weapon, ready for combat.

The stranger said, "We were only going to rob you, but now prepare to die, barbarian." He pulled a blade in one hand and a sickle in the other. Before Lark could do any damage, one of the blades from the stranger buried itself deep within the barbarian's right shoulder. As blood sprayed out, the barbarian brought his weapon around with one mighty blow and sliced the stranger in half, blood spraying all directions. Kindle and Dwindle, both working together, killed the stranger they were fighting.

The remaining stranger looked around and saw all his friends were dead. He turned to flee, but Amber shot him in the leg with an arrow. He fell to the ground, grasping his wound as he yelled in pain. The group walked over to him and saw Amber punching the man in the face, kicking his ribs, then she picked up a large rock and crushed his right knee. She then said in her own language, "This is what will happen to any who mess with me. Now the piece of slime cannot run."

Not a word was said as Dwindle took the pan from his head and knocked him out. Amber let out a giggle with blood dripping from her hands. Lark spoke, saying, "Good job, girl."

Amber pulled the weapon free from Lark's shoulder, and he laughed from the pain. Blood oozed from his wounds as Dwindle took care if his brother.

Mayflower said, "Someone should keep watch."

There was a loud crack of thunder with a flash of lightening from the sky. Kindle said, "I'll take first watch."

Lark told the group, "Amber said she will take next watch."

Kindle sat by the warm glow of the fire, fighting to stay awake, but losing the battle, he drifted off to slumber. Mayflower said, "It looks like I have first watch…"

After hours of listening to all the noise, Mayflower decided to cast a healing spell over them all. Soon, Amber jumped to the ground from a large boulder, letting Mayflower know she could get some sleep. Mayflower cast one more spell and fell silently to sleep.

To occupy her time, Amber sat throwing stones at the stranger, giggling. She noticed that he was healing, so she swiftly pulled a large knife and slit his throat. As his eyes grew wide, he gasped for air, and blood began to spray from his throat, covering Amber in a red mist as she let out a laugh. She turned and started skipping back to the fire while whistling a pleasant tune.

As she sat in the fires warm glow, she felt a rain drop on the back of her hand, and lighting lit the night sky. She could see the stranger being dragged off into the darkness. She gave an alarm, waking the group, pointing in that direction.

Dwindle found a hole in the side of a boulder. He was curious, so he looked inside and saw six red eyes looking back at him. Suddenly, a white web shot out, binding him. A huge brown spider with a red mark on its back crept forward dragging Dwindle towards the large hole. Lark ran over and slashed the sticky white web, getting his weapon stuck. Amber shot it once in an eye and then in the mouth. Kindle climbed up the side of the boulder with his war hammer. Mayflower cast a light spell inside the hole to draw the huge spider out. Kindle took a leap of faith, hoping his aim was right, and with a mighty blow from his war hammer, he crushed the spider's head, killing it instantly. Mayflower went to Dwindle's side to set him free. Using fire, it didn't take her long.

Soon, it began to pour down rain, so they took shelter from the storm. They all fell fast asleep, exhausted from their day's adventures. As the night began to chill, Amber curled up next to Lark for warmth and comfort as he pulled her close. The rest of the night was peaceful.

In the morning, Mayflower cast a light spell to inspect the shelter. In the back, she found three bodies wrapped in fine silk lying next to a pile of mixed bones and a silk sack filled with spider eggs ready to hatch. She recognized the stranger from the night before. Amber recognized the other two. She told Lark that they were from her village; they had been missing for two weeks, and she was out looking for them. Mayflower was worried about the spiders as they left the shelter. Mayflower threw a fireball on the fine silk, destroying everything that was left behind.

After their morning meal, Amber changed Lark's bandages, and they discovered he was completely healed. He jumped to his feet with an angry roar that got everyone's attention.

"You had no right woman! I despise magic! Why did you do this to me?"

Mayflower said, "Feeling better, are we? You're welcome."

Lark said, "Your magic is not welcome with me."

Mayflower said, "I only wanted to help, don't you feel better, big man?"

Lark replied, "I drew strength from my pain."

Mayflower said, "You were weak in your last battle. Amber took out three while you dispatched with only one, and she received no battle wounds."

Little Thief reached for her staff and received a strong jolt of electricity for his effort. Lark also reached down for the staff and received a jolt strong, enough to take him off his feet.

Dwindle slowly crept up behind the little ball of fur saying, "Yum, yum," as he picked up Little Thief. It let out a cry, and suddenly, Lark grabbed Dwindle by the throat and threw him over a large dead tree, landing in front of Mayflower. Mayflower took a step to the side, saying, "Let them have their fun!" The ladies kept walking. Kindle came charging around the dead tree, taking a swing at Lark and hitting him in his stomach. Lark let out an *oof* on impact. Lark recovered quickly and returned a blow to the side of Kindle's head, knocking him to one knee. Kindle let out a laugh as he stood up, saying, "Is that all you got?"

Without a warning, Dwindle jumped from the large dead tree with his frying pan in his hand making contact with the side of Lark's head, knocking him out for a moment. When Lark recovered from the blow, he picked up his little fuzzy friend, and putting him into his pouch without saying a word to Kindle or Dwindle, they all started to walk to catch up with Mayflower and Amber

Dwindle looked at his frying pan and found a dent from Lark's head. Dwindle said, "Me, me, brother, bang, *oof!*" as they both started laughing. Mayflower stopped in her tracks.

"I forgot my staff!" Within a flash, the staff appeared in her hand, and they continued to walk.

By midday, they reached a large and beautiful, blue, crystal lake. After hours of traveling together, they all smelled. Lark picked up Kindle and playfully threw him into the water, then took one look at Dwindle. Dwindle laughed and charged at Lark, knocking them both into the cold water. They had fun splashing each other. Mayflower decided to summon a large wave to soak all three. She and Amber were able to find a private spot to bathe in. Lark cleaned himself and Little Thief, who was not one-bit happy about getting wet.

After a quick meal, they noticed a poorly built raft. They all climbed aboard, hoping it would hold together. Lark stood in front with rope in hand and started pulling them across. With his muscles bulging when he flexed his back, Mayflower noticed Amber sitting behind Lark, staring with a look of desire in her eyes.

Halfway across the lake, a head emerged from the water. It was attached to a beautiful young mermaid, and within moments several more showed up. The first mermaid swam up to the raft to speak to the group.

"Kind people, we are in need of your help. Our greatest treasure has been taken from us and placed in a location that we cannot enter."

Mayflower answered, "Why should we help you? We have our own issues to deal with."

Lark told her to, "Sit down and shut up, or I'll throw you into the water."

The mermaids said, "Kind sir, you will be greatly rewarded," and she set a handful of blue diamonds at his feet, which got Little Thief's attention.

Mayflower said, "Very well. Have it your way. But the reward must be shared equally."

The mermaid said, "Our treasure is on that island," and pointed in that direction. "We will take you to the edge of the island. The rest is up to you. Our treasure is deep within its center."

Dwindle said, "Me, me, guard."

Kindle said, "We should split into two groups. Amber and Lark go that way. Mayflower and I will go this way. We will meet back here before sunset."

Kindle was not being as cautious as he should have been and set off a booby trap. Losing his balance, he fell into a pit.

Mayflower slowly looked over the edge and saw that he landed on a bed of small spikes. She was impressed that he didn't cry out. As she began to raise her hand, he arose from the pit to stand next to her as her power surged, and he began to heal.

At this time, Dwindle was playing with a turtle he had found. The mermaids looked on, singing a sweet, gentle song. There was a flash of light, and before Dwindle stood the most beautiful woman anyone had ever seen wearing a toga with a golden belt and a wreath of wildflowers in her hair. Dwindle was so fascinated playing with his turtle that this beautiful woman had gone unnoticed. She walked over and perched herself upon a boulder to watch Dwindle play like a child.

The brush started getting thick around Lark and Amber. Lark had to use his sword to cut away some of the brush. Behind a huge tree, half-buried, they found a chest. It took them a while to dig it out. Lark reached down and slung it over his broad shoulders to carry back. Amber followed behind, watching his every move while dreaming of a life together.

They all returned about the same time and saw this beautiful woman watching Dwindle. Kindle ran to protect his brother as Amber prepared her bow. The beautiful woman stood, saying, "I mean no harm."

Amber slipped and let lose an arrow, but this beautiful woman waved her hand, and the arrow vanished.

Mayflower spoke, asking, "Who are you?"

"I am Luna, goddess of stars and moons at night. This dwarf here is funny and amuses me."

Lark delivered the chest to the raft, so the mermaids could retrieve their queen's lost crown and scepter. The mermaids were filled with joy and placed a bag of jewels and a beautiful gold horn on the raft and said, "This is your reward, thank you."

Lark asked, "What is this?" pointing at the horn.

The mermaid replied, "In time of need, sound the horn."

The mermaid gently gave him a soft kiss in his cheek. Amber saw what had just taken place, and with anger in her eyes, she came marching over and scared the beautiful mermaid away, asking, "Why did she kiss you?"

Lark replied, "She just said thank you."

All the mermaids waved and slowly disappeared back into the water.

The goddess asked, "What is your quest?" Mayflower explained about everything, and Luna said, "There's a boat on the other side of this island for you to continue."

When they reached the other boat, Lark looked into the bag that the mermaids had given him, and his eyes grew wide. Without saying a word, Mayflower snatched the bag from his hand to look inside, and her eyes grew wide as well. She said, I've never seen so many pretty colors!"

At that moment, Amber reached for the bag, knocking it down and spilling out the precious jewels. They all looked in surprise at all the beautiful gems.

Lark said, "Amber, you stupid woman, look what you've done!"

As they were arguing no one noticed Little Thief dragging the bag away.

He delivered it at Luna's feet. She reached down and picked them both up, which ended the argument. Soon, they got off the boat and made camp for the night, but after their meal, Lark called them all over. Luna told the group, "It's time to split these among you."

Dwindle looked at the beautiful gems and said, "Wow, wow, mine."

Luna surprised the group when she spoke to Amber, telling her of her share. Amber told Luna, "I want none of it. He can have mine as she pointed at Lark."

Kindle said, "I shall hold onto my brothers and mine," as Dwindle said, "Me, me, brother."

Soon, they drifted into slumber with a loud rumble. Luna said, "Is this for real?" Mayflower cast her spell and laid down to rest. Luna said, "That does me non good. I can take care of this for good…." She raised her hand and lighting flew from her hand to the boys silencing their snores and casting them into a peaceful sleep.

The next morning, as the sun rose, the group awoke to a loud rumbling noise. Luna was fast asleep, snoring louder than any of the others ever had, shaking the boulders around her. They all stared at what was going on before their eyes.

Mayflower rose early and prepared a large meal. Luna awoke to find herself the center of attention. As she yawned and stretched, saying, "Mmm, that smells wonderful."

When they had finished their meal, they began their day's journey. In a short while, they came across some dead humans. Many were missing their heads, as these were displayed impaled on 10-foot stakes.

By midday, they came across another battlefield covered in blood with orcs and dead humans lying everywhere. Some were missing limbs; others, you could once again see them displayed on stakes. Gore was still fresh with blood dripping into pools.

They made their way across the battlefield stepping over broken and bloody weapons. They heard a weak voice and found a badly injured knight. He said, "Beware of the orcs."

Mayflower could see he was near death and cast a healing spell, but it was too late. Lark said, "The only good night is a dead knight," and he let out a chuckle, adding, "I fear no stinking orcs."

They heard some loud noises; a group of orcs marching a short distance away. Mayflower summoned a fog spell for them to take cover as they pulled out their weapons, getting ready for battle. Lark decided to run ahead of them to sit on the path to surprise them as they came around a bend.

There was a moment of confusion when the orcs stopped suddenly. The leader of the orcs fell as arrows rained from above. Orcs fired arrows into the tree tops, hitting Amber in the leg. She fell from the limb, landing on the ground and breaking her arm. Lark rushed in, swinging his war hammer crushing one orc's face spraying out warm, wet liquid. He rounded, hitting another and sinking his hammer into the orc's chest. His hammer was covered in blood and gore. Kindle swung his hammer like a club, crushing one orc's knee as Dwindle got sliced in his upper arm. Kindle came to his brother's side and was cut very deep as blood poured onto the ground from his leg.

Lark spotted an orc and charged. Their swords clashed with such force, both weapons shattered from the impact. He received an arrow in his shoulder for his effort, and blood oozed from his wound. Dwindle was able to throw his war hammer to Lark, so he could defend himself, but he hit Lark in the leg instead. Luna cast a spell of protection from fire over Lark and the brothers. Mayflower struck two orcs with a fireball. Out of nowhere, a cone of fire struck the orcs from behind, taking out many of them at the same time.

When the battle finished, the brothers, Lark, and Amber inspected their battle wounds. Deep within the depth of the surrounding darkness emerged a dark beast that stood six-foot-tall and 12 feet long.

Luna said, "I blew the horn which summoned Shadow."

As he looked over the messed-up group, he drummed his nine-inch steel claws on the ground. Luna spoke to Shadow, saying, "Their hearts are pure, and their quest is noble."

Within moments, Luna snapped her fingers and summoned a healing spell over the whole group, except for Amber's broken arm. When Amber appeared from the woods with her broken arm, Shadow walked up to Amber and said, "I can heal you." As he opened up his mouth showing eight-inch teeth dripping with healing acid, Amber was shocked to hear this cat talk. He said, "Raise your arm. Don't be frightened," as he gently bit down to heal her arm.

"Thank you for your kindness," Amber said.

Amber and Mayflower noticed a very soft saddle on Shadow's back that was made to carry two people. Shadow asked, "Would you ladies like to ride?"

They answered, "Yes please," and Shadow lowered himself, so they could climb on.

By midday, the path came to a halt at a wall of rock. They looked up and found a cave about 100 feet up. Shadow told the ladies, "Hold on, I got this," as his large claws came out. He was able to climb the sheer face up to the cave entrance.

"I'm tired, I need to eat and rest," he told them. He spoke a magic word, and suddenly, a pile of food appeared next to the pile of bones.

Mayflower said, "We must get everyone up here."

Amber went to the edge and sat down with a drumstick in her hand. She looked down and could not see anyone. She turned to Shadow, and everyone was eating the food.

Lark said, "I told, you stupid woman, I despise your magic! First you heal me again, then you bring me up here."

Mayflower said, "I did nothing.

Luna said, "I cast a protection spell, then I healed you."

Shadow said, "I brought everyone up here. Do you have a problem with that, boy?"

Luna said, "Shadow is a powerful wizard and does whatever he wants. He is stronger than any of you. If I was you, Lark, I would keep my mouth shut."

Mayflower said, "I am new to this type of magic. Can you please help me?"

Luna turned to Shadow and asked, "Would you like to help her?"

Shadow called Mayflower over to sit by his side. As he blinked his eyes, he unlocked all the hidden secrets of magic within her mind. He said, "That should do it." He saw a ledge 40 feet higher and climbed up for a cat nap.

The group slowly entered the cave. Mayflower noticed that Lark and the brothers could not see in total darkness. She cast a globe of light that would follow them. As they ventured deeper into the cave, they suddenly stopped short from falling into a deep hole. Lark stepped back, ran, and leaped over it. Luna teleported everyone else to the other side.

As they continued, they found broken shields and weapons with bones littering the cave floor. They entered a large, open cavern that was piled high with treasure. They stood overlooking a large pile of gold and weapons. A stair at one side disappeared into the pile of treasure.

They decided to replace their broken and missing weapons. Mayflower sifted through the pile. She came across a unique quarter staff with runes engraved on it and a large sapphire embedded in the top. She felt the power before she touched it. She knew it was for her.

A huge black dragon landed at the mouth of the cave. He heard noises from within his cave. He could smell the stink of intruders. He immediately changed form into a human and slowly began to make his way down to his chamber. He watched the group plundering his beautiful prized positions. He grew very angry and jumped down to the base of his treasure, saying, "How dare you thieves to come in to my home and steal my things!" Without a warning he transformed back into a huge black dragon.

Amber turned with such speed and let loose four arrows with her new bow that struck him in his chest, which only angered hm. The twins charged with their new axes. The black dragon turned, swatting Kindle with his powerful tail and slamming him to the ground, shattering his bones. As Kindle crumpled on the pile of gold, Dwindle rushed over to help his brother, but he was too late. He took a swing at the black dragon with his new battle axe. The black dragon caught him by the arm, picked him up, and started viciously shaking him. Then he slammed him to the ground and stepped on his head while ripping his arm off at the elbow. Blood began to pool around his lifeless body.

Amber spotted a weakness on the black dragon and told Lark. They both rushed in. The black dragon used his powerful wings to blast air, blowing them both back as they slid down the pile of gold. Amber took off running in one direction while Lark took off running in the other, trying to confuse the beast. The black dragon was focused on Amber and leaped in front of her, blocking her path. The black dragon tried to bite her, but she was too quick for him. She fired two arrows, but they just bounced off of him. Lark was able to get close and took a swing at the black dragon's weakness. Blood gushed from the wound as the beast turned, blowing out a cone of fire, killing him where he stood. Amber ran up the dragon's back, pulling out her blades as she ran. She tried to stab the beast on top of the head but was caught in the dragons' mighty jaws. She was thrown against a wall and fell in a lifeless pile next to Luna.

Mayflower felt a great power from staff as it began to glow matching her eyes. A vision appeared in her mind as she began to transform into a small sapphire dragon. Luna said, "She's going to need some help…" then went off to get Shadow.

Mayflower charged and blew a cone of frost towards the huge black dragon. The huge dragon blew fire towards Mayflower, making her attack pointless. He overpowered her, causing some of her scales to fly off.

Mayflower ran in and collided with him, fighting fiercely with long claws and sharp teeth. They both received serious injuries as blood flowed from the open wounds. The huge dragon started to overpower Mayflower, causing more injuries as she was knocked to the floor.

Shadow and Luna entered the room and witnessed the huge black dragon jump up and down on top of her, pinning her down with great force. He bit down ripping a chunk of flesh from her neck. Blood began to spill onto the ground. He then blew fire onto the wound as flesh and blood sprayed into the air. He let out a roar of victory.

Shadow mumbled a word, and in that instant, a suit of battle armor appeared on him. The armor transformed him into a deadly weapon. He crept forward, getting close enough to pounce. He landed in front of the huge black dragon striking out with his large claws and ripping his chest open. The black dragon roared in pain as blood oozed down his front side. The dragon swatted Shadow, causing him to tumble. Shadow recovered to strike again.

Shadow jumped on top of the black dragon, ripping and tearing the back of the neck as blood gushed out. The dragon rolled over to free himself as Shadow jumped off. Before he could land, he was hit by the dragon's tail. Pieces of armor flew off of Shadow. Shadow jumped up, clawing and biting his neck, again ripping more flesh from an already open wound. As blood once again poured out, weakening the huge beast, he tried to breathe fire that had no effect on Shadow. Again, Shadow pounced on the huge beast and ripped once more at the gaping wound, severing the huge beast's head. Blood pumped out spraying everywhere.

Luna said, "They still need your help."

Shadow walked up to Mayflower as Luna gathered the bodies of the others. He leaned over and gently bit Mayflower. She began to heal, and she transformed back to her normal self. She was very weak but managed to sit up to look at this beautiful battle cat.

Shadow said, "Next time, pick a fight you can win young lady." Mayflower laughed. Shadow asked, "Where are the others?"

Luna said, "I placed the bodies over there."

Shadow felt proud at what he had accomplished and strutted over to their bodies. Luna and Shadow together started casting major healing spells. Shadow laid on the ground as Luna laid the bodies around him. He began to glow as his energy spread out among them all.

In a few minutes, they began to breathe again. As the glow began to fade, they slowly sat up as Luna pointed to Lark and Amber, saying, "They are the reason I am here."

Kindle looked around and saw Little Thief sitting at his feet with his belt pouch. Kindle gently picked him up. Dwindle was saying, "Me, me, food, brother."

Kindle said, "No! This is our friend, not food."

Luna talked to Lark and Amber about living with her. Together, they looked at each other and smiled, both saying, "Yes, thank you," as Amber gave Shadow a soft hug. Shadow opened a portal and Luna, Amber, and Lark stepped through it together. The brothers spoke together, saying, "We miss our home."

Mayflower cast another spell, and they vanished. Shadow laid down for Mayflower to climb into his soft saddle to continue her quest.

They slowly went deeper into the cave to find an exit on the other side. They emerged to find themselves on the edge of a thousand-foot drop overlooking the cloud forest. Mayflower said, "It's late, let's get some rest."

They watched the sunset as they shared a meal together. Shadow fell fast asleep, and Mayflower laid down against his beautiful soft fur. She watched the stars and the moon until she drifted into a deep sleep.

The next morning, they woke up, and Shadow stretched and yawned. He said, "Get on, let's go," as she sat down in the soft saddle holding her new staff. He said, "Here we go!" and he jumped over the edge to run down the side of the cliff. Forty feet from the ground, he leaped out from the wall landing on top of an orc, killing it as he sprayed a cone of fire from his mouth, killing the remaining few orcs that were there.

Shadow saw a wild boar, and without a warning, he took off chasing it, playing with his food before he killed it. Mayflower screamed like a frightened child when he stopped to eat his kill. Mayflower climbed down on unsteady legs. She found her voice and said, "I thought we were going to die. Don't ever do that to me again!"

Shadow laughed with a mouth full of raw meat and replied, "That ain't nothing, young lady. You were never in any danger." And he turned to finish his meal. He said, "Oops, I forgot my manners. Would you like some?"

Mayflower said, "No thank you, you finish your meal."

When he was done, he asked, "Are you ready, young lady?"

She climbed up and sat down. Shadow took off running at full speed.

By midday, they reached a canyon 250 feet wide. As Shadow leaped, Mayflower looked down at an army of orcs camped out by a river. She wondered if he would make it to the other side. He cleared the jump easily and continued running.

By sunset, they came to the edge of a cliff. As they looked down, they saw a small village with families milling about. Shadow spotted a little girl crying, holding a teddy bear that was missing a leg. Shadow teleported the little girl up to the cliff with them and said, "Don't be afraid, we will help."

She handed her bear to Mayflower and said, "Please fix."

Mayflower looked up at Shadow, as he nodded his head. Mayflower took out a needle and thread and started repairing the child's toy. When she was finished, Shadow gave her an extremely beautiful doll as a gift. The child ran over and gave Shadow a gentle hug, saying "Pretty kitty."

Shadow asked the young lady, "What is your name, precious?"

"My name is Mars."

Shadow said, "May I ask you another question Mars? How old are you?"

"I'm almost seven years old."

Shadow asked, "Would you like to be my friend?"

"I would love that, pretty kitty."

"My name is Shadow. If you ever need me, just call my name."

She said, "How old are you, pretty kitty?"

"I'm 6,048 years old." Mayflower and Mars both said, "Wow…" very slowly at the same time. "Now it's time for you to go home, young lady," and he sent her back to her village.

They decided to rest for the night. The next morning, Mayflower looked out across the valley and saw a black fog rolling across the valley floor, devouring everything it touched.

The small village was sitting right in its path. Before she could say a word, Shadow cast a teleportation spell, and she appeared between the village and the black fog.

The black fog appeared with two large red eyes. It spoke, saying, "Puny little fairy, you can't stop me, for I have devoured many of your kind."

As the black fog crept towards her, Mayflower looked at her staff and noticed it was glowing dark blue.

Shadow was on the cliff overlooking the scene. A matching, dark blue glow formed around him. He cast his greatest spells into her staff. She yelled to the black fog, "I will do one thing that no other has done before!" She raised her staff and said, "You are done here for good!" She brought down her staff, shattering its magical gem against a boulder. A brilliant light of pure good exploded around her, destroying the dark fog along with the beast that lived within it.

Shadow leaped into the air from the cliff, casting a blink spell, and appeared next to her lifeless body.

He immediately called Grunch. Grunch appeared and noticed that his friend gave all his spells into a broken staff. He knew what had just taken place. He told Shadow, "Her sacrifice was noble. I shall reward her, and you as well. Come now, it's time to go home."

Grunch gently picked up Mayflower and all three vanished. The villagers slowly came out of hiding, and they knew their lives would be safe.

2

THE UNDEAD

When Grunch and Shadow appeared back home, Grunch carried a limp body in his arms. They were greeted by a six-foot tall dragon that went by the name of Zanlue and was dressed in a blue robe with golden runes and wearing thick glasses. Zanlue, being curious, asked, "What is her name?"

Grunch said, "Her name is Mayflower. Prepare a room for this beautiful lady, treat her like royalty with highest respect OR ELSE! Prepare a beautiful room six levels up, just beyond the double golden doors."

As he opened the doors, the aroma of fresh roses could be smelled throughout the room. A large, soft bed sat off to the right with an oak table next to it. There was a blue candle burning and a fresh bowl of fruit on the table. To the left sat a phoenix resting on its perch.

Grunch walked to the bed and gently set Mayflower down. As this went on, Zanlue, in a rumbling voice, said, "Wake up, you stupid, lazy bird. You have a job to do." He picked up a stick to poke at the bird, saying, "Get to work! This person needs to be healed now!"

The phoenix replied, "I'm not as stupid as you are dumb-dumb. Why don't you heal her?"

Zanlue shot back, "That's your job, you stupid, flaming, lazy bird."

Grunch turned and said, "One of you—heal her now!"

The phoenix told Grunch, "Heal her yourself, you big brute."

Grunch marched over to the phoenix, grabbed him by the neck, and started shaking him. Feathers flew in all directions. Zanlue tried not to laugh, but his grin was obvious.

Shadow appeared by the side of the bed. Grunch released the bird and returned to Mayflower's bedside. Shadow said, "I'll heal her," putting his huge paws on the soft bed next to her. He bent down and mumbled some strange words.

Within minutes, Mayflower took her first breath. She opened her eyes and was surprised to see Shadow's big head only inches from her face. She gave him a loving embrace as he gently wrapped his huge paws around her and said, "You are safe now."

A tear of joy ran down her face as she said, "Thank you."

Grunch said, "You must rest now, Shadow will stay to keep you company."

The phoenix said, "I'll keep watch."

Shadow replied, "Go find something to do." The phoenix flew out the window, and Shadow continued, "You my friend, don't you have your books to study?"

Zanlue said, "Very well. It's nice to meet you, Mayflower."

Mayflower laid back down and drifted off to sleep. Grunch said, "I must go now, I have need of those brothers Kindle and Dwindle..." Then, he vanished.

Suddenly, a small grappling hook appeared through the window and began to slowly move toward the sill. With a jerk, it caught on tight. Shadow went to the window and looked down; he saw a small halfling busily climbing the silk rope attached to the grappling hook. He backed up to wait patiently, drumming his claws on the floor. When she reached the window, Shadow got up to meet her. They were face to face when Shadow said, "Hellooo..." and licked the side of her face. She was shocked at what had just happened. She slid down the rope as fast as she could. When she reached the bottom, you could hear a scream as she ran off.

Grunch appeared a mile from the town of the dwarfes. He started walking, and after a short while, he came across an old dwarf with a cart full of weapons covered with a tarp that had a broken wheel. He began to talk with the old dwarf. His wife had just died, and he had lost his faith. Grunch said, "Don't give up on the gods yet. Maybe it was just her time."

The old man said, "I prayed, and I prayed. I miss her terribly."

Grunch asked, "What would you do if you ever meet a god?"

The old man said, "I would worship him for the rest of my life and beyond."

Grunch picked up the back end of the cart, so the old man could fix the wheel. When the wheel was off, Grunch let go, crushing the old man's hand.

Grunch said, "I'm sorry, but it had to be done." He then showed the old man his true form. Grunch said, "Your sacrifice was necessary to bring her back."

As he looked up, the old man saw a fog drifting in and his wife walking toward him. He forgot about his crash as he ran to embrace his wife with tears of joy running down his face. She could only ask, "How?" He turned back toward Grunch, but he had vanished, and the cart was repaired.

As Grunch entered the town of Timire, people were out and about with their daily activities. Grunch soon found the tavern he was looking for and went in. As he looked around, he found a table in a corner. He walked over and sat down, leaning back in the chair with his massive arms crossed, and waited patiently. A halfling barmaid came to Grunch's table, and she said, "My name is Crystal, what can I bring you?"

"I'll take whatever you bring me, young lady."

She brought him a large steak with a pitcher of cold beer.

She returned after his meal, and he asked Crystal to sit and talk. She replied, "I'd be very honored, Grunch. I know who you are. There are many legends about you here. I won't tell anyone you're here."

He asked, "What is your favorite color?"

She said, "Blue and pink," so he dropped a handful of blue and pink diamonds on her tray.

Her beautiful blue eyes grew wide as she said, "Thank you, kind sir," then she turned and ran off.

Suddenly, a half-breed thought it would be funny to trip this young lady. That angered Crunch. He stood up, saying, "Try that with me, you half breed troll!" as he stepped forward.

The half-breed answered, "Very well then."

Within a blink of an eye, Grunch picked him up by his throat with one hand driving him through a wooden table with such force, you could hear his bones snap. Before Grunch could do anything else, he saw a dwarf with green hair wearing a frying pan on his head run and bounce off the belly of the largest human. Kindle went to his brother's side, looked at the largest human, and threw a punch at the man who was standing next to him. The fighting had begun.

Grunch grabbed another half breed as a wooden stool was smashed over his back with great force. He lost his grip and staggered forward when a beer mug was broken over his head, leaving a very deep and bloody gash as blood dripped down from his face.

Kindle and Dwindle were finishing up with their opponent. Suddenly, one of the humans went flying over their heads and through the wall, landing in a crumpled pile outside with a broken neck as an old friend named Stew, a minotaur with speed, kicked another man over the table, which disturbed a party of four ogres. An angry ogre grabbed Dwindle, lifting him up over his head, and threw him through another wooden table, breaking his right arm.

Grunch was standing next to him and heard the bone snap. He hit the ogre with a war hammer that appeared in his hand. The ogre's right leg shattered with pieces of bone sticking out from the impact, spraying blood onto the floor. The ogre dropped in pain, and the hammer vanished. Stew saw this happen, and guided by his natural hatred for ogres, he began to focus solely on them while Grunch was busy fighting the rest. It didn't take long for the floor to be littered with bloody bodies and broken furniture. In the end, the only one standing was Stew.

At that moment, the door burst open, and peace keepers in suits of chainmail with long swords in their hands filled the room. As Stew's favorite weapon, his double-bladed battle axe, a gift from Grunch, appeared in his hands. He looked over at Grunch and smiled. Stew started to swing his battle axe, hitting the peace keepers one after another. He decapitated two, and cut one in half, then buried his battle axe in the chest on another. Before Stew could pull it free, several more peace keepers entered the room. There was a wizard watching the action from the left who cast a spell, knocking Stew out.

The peace keepers took everyone to jail. The cells filled quickly with all three involved in the fight. Stew was placed in a cage just outside the jail. In the cell over was a single dark elf. Grunch spoke to him, asking, "Who are you?"

"I'm Scar, and I will surely be put to death for slicing the throat of that evil tax collector."

The cell across from them held five beaten-up humans. Kindle taunted them, saying, "*Boom, crash, ahh!* Stupid humans," as he and his brother Dwindle pointed a finger at them and laughed. The smallest human spoke, saying, "What kind of dwarfs are you? I've never seen fighting like that."

Before Grunch could answer. Dwindle said, "Man, *bang, bang,* Grunch!" pointing at the largest human.

Finally, Grunch answered, "We are just some travelers."

Grunch turned to Kindle and asked, "Who are you?"

"My name is Kindle, and this is my brother Dwindle. You'll have to excuse him. He's not normal."

Grunch said, "I've been looking for you two, would you come with me to my home? Some friends of yours are there. You know Mayflower and Shadow. We have much to discuss."

Grunch called for the guard to ask, "How much would it cost to pay for all the damages and to free all of us?"

The guard answered, "You can't possibly afford it."

Grunch repeated, "How much will it be?"

The guard said, "It's 250,000, except for the minotaur in the cage outside."

Grunch said, "Very well." Then, he snapped his fingers, and a very large, red ruby appeared. "This will take care of all costs."

The guard was amazed and asked, "Who are you?"

"I am Grunch, god of rampage. You are wearing my insignia on your cloak." The guard dropped to his knees and began to worship him. "No need for that. You were doing your job."

The small man named John heard this and said, "I've heard legends about a dwarf killing over 300 dragons. That sounds like you. What are you doing here?"

Grunch replied, "I've come to get these two. I can tell your heart is pure, would you like to be one of my followers?"

John said, "My lovely wife is ill, and I don't know if she will make it. I need money for my family, I would like to, but I don't see how it's possible."

Grunch said, "I'll make it possible for you. What is the weapon of your choice?"

John said, "I've been trained with all kinds of blades. I'm best with a sword, but I cannot afford a good one."

The largest human spoke up and said, "You want this puny, weak man to be your follower? I'm three times his size, you should choose me."

Grunch said, "Shut up, puny man! Your heart is not pure like his."

Before John could say anything else, there appeared a suit of gold plate nail with a cloak with his insignia on it, a sack of jewels, and a beautiful, ancient long sword with runes engraved on the blade and a large ruby imbedded in its handle. He said, "These are for you, John."

John asked, "How do you know my name?"

Grunch said, "I'm a god." He pointed to the large man and said, "I know what you are thinking. Keep your hands off."

The guard unlocked all the cells except for Scar's. As they all walked out. Grunch noticed Scar's door remained locked. Grunch walked over to Scar's door, and without a word, he put his hands on the locked door and pulled it off its hinges. He said, "Follow me." The guard stepped aside.

When they stepped outside, Stew was still locked in a cage with eight guards standing watch. Grunch walked over and said, "He is coming with us."

A guard walked over to Grunch and said, "We know who you are. We don't want any trouble." Grunch snapped his fingers, and Stew was standing next to him.

Stew said, "Thank you, old friend. This was fun, but I have to go home now," as he turned and walked.

John said, "You are all welcome to rest in my home."

When they arrived, his wife and two daughters were busy preparing a meal. He was surprised to see her up and well. She said, "I just woke up feeling better. I heard a soft voice in my head saying, 'Prepare a meal, you'll have company.'"

They all sat down to fill their bellies. Afterwards, they sat by the warm fire to talk.

John pulled out his beautiful ancient long sword to inspect it. His wife dropped a handful of plates and fell to her knees looking at that beautiful sword. She could not believe her eyes.

"How did you receive a death ringer? I heard the stories of the lost swords when I was a child. I thought it was only a myth about these beautiful powerful swords that a god made… They really do exist!"

John said, "That's not all," as she stood up. He handed her a bag of jewels. She opened the bag, and her eyes grew wide. She staggered back and fell into a beautiful, soft chair.

John asked Grunch to tell him about this weapon.

"There are only 12 lost swords that exist. This is, indeed, a death ringer, as your wife says. Its powers are beyond belief. Many people will try to take this beautiful sword from you. Protect it well."

John's wife asked, "Who are you?"

"I'm the god of rampage."

She was speechless. Scar spoke up and said, "I'm in your debt."

Grunch said, "We need your skills on a quest."

Kindle sat down and removed the pouch from his side. A little head popped out and looked around, then a ball of fur ran to the table to get a piece of bread. Dwindle jumped up and said, "Me, me, food, food!" and ran after him.

His brother said, "No food, he's our friend."

Dwindle grabbed a piece of bread and said, "Me, me, food, food," as the others started to laugh. They all settled down and rested for the night.

As they were sleeping, Grunch was sitting by the warm fire. John's wife Tina came over and sat by him. She asked, "Are you the one that healed me?"

"Yes." Before she could even ask the question, he said, "You and your family will always be protected." Grunch asked, "Would you like to come with me? I have something to show you."

She said, "Okay," and they both vanished.

They reappeared in a giant cavern. Sitting on a throne was a huge, giant-size man with red hair and a long beard. Grunch told her, "His name is Big Red. He is a northern Viking, and a very good friend of mine."

As Big Red sat on his throne with his pet spiders crawling all over him, he said, "Hello you two, I knew you two would be here soon. I could sense your presence coming, and you young lady, I know all about you, Tina. You may go over there and inspect each sword."

She said, "Thank you," and she hurried over toward the swords filled with joy as Grunch and Big Red talked with each other.

In a short time, they heard a loud squeal of excitement coming from her direction. Big Red said, "She found them."

As she picked them up, she heard a soft voice in her head telling her the name of each sword. After she inspected all of the beautiful swords, she returned to Grunch and Big Red and said, "I am honored to be here, thank you. I'll never forget this."

Grunch looked at Big Red with a grin. Big Red said, "I know what you're thinking. Wound Maker would be perfect for her."

Grunch snapped his fingers and transported Wound Maker into her hands. She held this beautiful sword made of silver with ancient runes on the blade with a large white diamond embedded into the handle. Grunch said, "This one is yours." She squealed again, as she could not hold back her excitement. She ran up to each of them giving them a hug.

Big Red removed a gold ring from his little finger and handed it to her. He said, "Any time you feel threatened, just call out, and one of us will come."

She put the huge ring on her finger. It automatically adjusted to fit perfectly.

Grunch said, "It's time to go now," and they both reappeared back at the warm fire with her beautiful sword in her hand. She got up and said goodnight, and she carried her beautiful sword into her room.

In the morning, Grunch awoke early and prepared a huge breakfast. The first to arrive were the two little girls. One of the girls asked, "Why do you look so funny?"

He scratched his head and said, "It's a long, long story, trust me. Which one of you would be willing to do me a favor?"

The oldest one spoke, "What do you need, funny looking man?"

"My friend had something that needs to be cared for."

She jumped with joy, asking, "Is it that little pet?"

"He's no pet, he is a friend."

Both little girls were happy about it and said, "Yes!" immediately.

When John and Tina showed up for breakfast, Tina brought her new sword for John to see. She said, "Look here at what I got!"

He asked, "Where did that beautiful sword come from?"

Grunch said, "Last night we took a little trip to a friend of mine. This last sword is a gift for her." As the others showed up for breakfast, Grunch told John, "Your girls will be watching after Little Thief while we are gone. I would like to reward them for doing this."

John replied, "Give them what you think is fair."

Grunch said, "I hope they will enjoy their gifts."

When the girls went to their rooms, half the room was piled with all sorts of toys and dolls, and there was a small chest filled with beautiful jewelry. Another chest appeared on John's wife dressing table, also filled with beautiful jewelry as well. The girls were filled with joy. Each ran to give Grunch a hug.

Grunch said, "It's time to go."

As they gathered their things together, Stew arrived and asked, "Can you use another hand?"

"Yes," Grunch replied as they all vanished.

They reappeared in a large dining hall in Grunch's home. They saw that Mayflower had the phoenix by the neck and was shaking him violently, causing feathers to fly.

Kindle ran to her and pulled her from the bird. Grunch asked, "What's going on here?"

She said, "That stupid bird called me a witch. I'm no witch!"

Zanlue said, "I told you, you stupid, dumb bird, you can't insult her like that!"

She went to pout and noticed the brothers. That put a smile on her face as she gave each a hug. Out of the corner of her eye, she saw Stew and froze. She didn't know what to think of a minotaur in the room. Grunch sat at the head of a large table, saying, "Everyone, come and sit. We have much to discuss, but we still need one another."

Big Red appeared in a chair at the table and said, "Here we go again, my old friend."

As everyone watched, Stew picked up his chair and placed it next to Mayflower. She sat straight up and stared at Grunch.

Grunch said, "Introductions are in order, everyone will introduce yourself and tell the others what spirits you bring along with you."

Mayflower felt more at ease around Stew. She asked Grunch, "Did he really win his freedom as a gladiator?"

Grunch said, "He did that and so much more."

Stew gently patted her on the back and said, "Good friends now?" as Dwindle said, "*Moo.*"

Grunch spoke, saying, "Now I will tell you why you are all here. We must retrieve a shard from the black crystal. The dead are not at rest; we must return the shard to the crystal, so it can be destroyed. No one knows where the shard is."

Mayflower cleared her throat as she pulled a gem from her blue robe and asked, "Is this the gem that you're talking about? I found it in a small chest from one of the rooms we were practicing magic in. I thought it looked pretty, Shadow told me I can keep it." She dropped the pretty gem, and it slid to the middle of the table, stood on end, and began to spin.

An insignificant little demon appeared on the table and said, "This is a warning, I will destroy any who come for the crystal, starting with you, dark elf!" The demon waved his arm and mumbled some words as he faded back into the crystal gem.

Scar started to shake, and his head exploded, sending pieces of flesh and blood in every direction. The gem stopped spinning and laid back down.

Mayflower said, "I want to learn that spell." They all looked at her and she said, "What? That's a good spell to know."

Grunch said, "Now we need another person to disarm the traps."

Dwindle said, "Me, me, brother, no go—too spooky."

Grunch said, "Don't worry little friends, your jobs are to run this place. We must go to the armory and prepare ourselves." They followed Grunch to a very big hallway. Grunch said, "You must stay close. I'll show you why…"

He set off the deadly traps. Without warning, blades sliced through the air, and spikes embedded themselves into the floor as they reset themselves. He said, "Do exactly what I do: step, step, hop, twirl, all the way down to the heavy oak door at the end of the hall."

As they entered the armory, Grunch said, "Take the weapon of your choice."

They looked around and saw weapons in all directions, even on the ceiling. Mayflower found a short sword that fit her well. Stew sniffed each weapon he picked up and chose a double-bladed battle axe. Big Red looked around and noticed a great long sword, then he looked up, and stuck to the ceiling was his favorite weapon: a two-handed claymore. He grinned and called Grunch over and pointed up.

Grunch said, "Good choice, now figure out how to get it down." He looked around and found a 50-foot silk rope attached to a small hook. It took him many tries before he was able to retrieve his weapon.

Dwindle watched this and said, with excitement, "Me, me, *oof!* Stupid rope!" The brothers started to laugh at the Vikings misfortune. The brothers kept some leather armor with war axes.

Grunch gathered everyone together. He told them, "All these weapons and armor have been enchanted thousands of years ago. Prepare yourselves, go and rest; there is much to do tomorrow."

They all vanished and were transported to their rooms.

Grunch went to the tallest tower with a vest of sharp daggers and a plate of food. He waited a very long time for the little halfling who loved to climb. When she appeared in the window, she peaked in slowly to make sure there was no giant cat waiting for her. She saw Grunch instead and entered the room. Grunch said, "Light Foot, you are very difficult to keep track of. Please come and have a seat."

Grunch told her about the crystal. She said, "Okay, but you will owe me a big favor—and that ring you have on."

As he removed his ring, he vanished.

Next, he went to the stables and picked out two large war horses for Big Red and Stew.

Before the brothers could rest, Kindle found Shadow sitting on a ledge overlooking the dark blue sea. Kindle let him know that his brother's arm was broken and asked if he could help. Shadow said, "That will be easy," and gently bit down on Dwindle's arm. It began to heal. The brothers said, "Thank you!" and went back to their rooms to rest.

A few hours later, they all heard two loud explosions. Everyone came running to find out what had happened. They saw Zanlue come out of the potions room with his robe still smoking. Zanlue said, "I almost had it that time!" Everybody went back to bed.

A short time later Zanlue entered Mayflower's room and woke her up by poking her with a stick. He said, "Get up, help me now. I have a test coming up, and I can't get this potion right."

She was not happy about being awoken like that. She told him, "No! Go away!" And her eyes began to glow dark blue.

He asked, "What's wrong with your eyes?"

She said, "Leave now! Or else!"

He said, "Or else what?"

He flew backwards out of her room, and the door slammed shut. Grunch appeared in the hall in time to witness this incident. He shook his head and walked past, saying, "You're never going to learn, are you?" as he entered his room, closing the door behind him.

In the morning, Grunch was the first to arrive at the stables. He prepared the saddles for Shadow and the horses. Night Crawler was next to show up. Grunch cast a spell that protected her legs with blades and, her body with armor that matched his own. Light Foot came in and asked, "What am I going to ride?"

Grunch answered, "They'll be here shortly."

She saw Night Crawler and said, "Good morning, you look beautiful with your armor on."

Night crawler replied, "Thank you, Light Foot."

Big Red arrived next and went to talk with Night Crawler. They had a friendly conversation between two old friends. Stew was next to arrive and looked over the war horses and said, "This one is mine."

Shadow and Mayflower appeared at last. Light Foot took one look at Shadow and took off running away. Shadow pointed in front of her blocking her exit. He gently pushed her down with one of his mighty paws, then picked her up by the back of her shirt like a small kitten. He pranced back with her dangling from his mouth. She had her arms crossed and was not happy about this beast treating her in such a manner.

Grunch said, "This is Shadow, he will protect you."

Light Foot and Mayflower asked, "Grunch, what are you going to ride?"

He did not answer but said, "It's time to go now."

Stew and Big Red mounted their war horses.

Shadow laid down for Mayflower and Light Foot to climb into his beautiful soft seat saddle. Grunch then climbed up onto Night Crawler, as she got excited and whispered, "Yessss…" They all looked kind of intimidated by Grunch, as he looked menacing.

He waved his hand, and a portal opened before them. Grunch was first to go, followed by the rest. They appeared in a meadow in the middle of forest surrounded by mountains with peaks that reached high into the clouds. Big Red asked, "What direction do we go?"

Mayflower said, "North," as her eyes began glowing.

They started off traveling north. In the distance, they saw movement. As they got closer, they saw that these were four zombies. Big Red said, "I'll take care of these creatures, I've dealt with them before."

He galloped off to battle. As he jumped off his war horse, he beheaded each of them with mighty blows from his claymore. The group caught up, and Big Red said, "I guess that was all of them."

At that moment, an undead Minotaur charged with great power, sinking both of his great horns deep into the side of Big Red's war horse, knocking it over onto him, breaking Big Reds right leg. Stew jumped off his war horse, swinging his battle axe and burying it deep into the neck of the undead creature, finishing it off. Grunch came forward and climbed off Night Crawler as she shot a web on the horse and pulled if off Big Red's broken leg and began to feast on the large dead animal. Shadow cast a healing spell to heal Big Red's leg. Grunch told the group, "You'll have nothing to worry about as long as you don't die."

With Big Red on foot, the group traveled slowly. By midday they came across a run-down castle and decided to would be a good place to have a meal and get some rest After their meal, they spread out. Mayflower sat on a tarp next to a pile of straw and noticed something shinny inside the pile. She uncovered a dark crystal ball, and at that moment, a dark wizard and a warlock appeared. Shadow walked up to Mayflower, and he told her prepare for battle.

The warlock said, "I remember you well, Shadow. You killed my brother and put this scar across my face. This time, I will destroy you."

Grunch appeared from nowhere and said, "This fight is between you four. No-one else will interfere, I want to see what Shadow has taught you, Mayflower." He then walked to a broken wall and leaned against it with his arms crossed to watch.

The wizard wanted to test Grunch by throwing a fireball at him. Grunch just swatted the fireball away. Having no effect, Grunch said, "Trust me, your fight is with them, not with me."

Suddenly, a black fireball shot past Mayflower as she stood next to Shadow. Mayflower took four steps over and launched a six-foot boulder forward, missing the wizard and shattering the wall behind him. At that moment, a lightning bolt struck shadows right shoulder. The warlock laughed. Shadow decided to summon a hail storm that would cover a one-mile area, and the sky grew dark. The wizard waved his hand, and within moments Mayflower yelled in pain as a deep gash appeared across her chest with blood oozing out. Seconds later, Shadow summoned a spell that would shoot ice spikes, striking them both. As holes were being ripped open across their bodies, blood began to drip onto the battleground. A couple seconds later, Mayflower held up her hand and a ray of starlight burst forth from her head, hitting them both as well. Pieces of their flesh pealed from their bodies as they cried out in pain.

Before the wizard or the warlock could react, large hail stones started falling from the sky, pelting everyone. They all took cover except for Grunch, who just stayed on his spot. As everyone else was waiting for the storm to pass, Mayflower used the time to heal both of them, and talk. The wizard also healed them both, and suddenly the wizard reappeared right in front of Grunch. Grunch said, "What is it that you want?"

The wizard asked, "Why is it you travel with these unworthy people?"

"They are my friends." Grunch snapped his fingers and sent him back.

As the storm stopped, the warlock put away his spell book, and they both walked back to finish their battle with Shadow and Mayflower. Mayflower and Shadow appeared before Grunch. Grunch told them, "You know what you have to do, so do it."

Mayflower said, "Let's finish this."

Suddenly shards of spikes hit them both across their backs as blood dripped onto the ground. Mayflower got very angry and turned around and yelled, "Really, are you kidding me?"

She summoned a storm of deadly blades, holding them in place 20 feet above their heads, the wizard held up his hand, and shot out a magic missile that struck Mayflower in the chest, exploding on impact and knocking her down hard with blood oozing out from the hole in her chest. She lost concentration, and the storm of deadly blades fell onto the wizard and the warlock. Only the wizard was able to survive the attack. They noticed a glow around the wizard, and the deadly blades shattered on impact.

The warlock laid crumpled on the ground with blades covering his bloody body. Grunch saw what had just taken place and could see that the wizard was now wearing a ring of protection. In the wizard's mind, he heard a soft voice telling him that this needed to be a fair fight. As the ring vanished from his finger to reappear in Grunch's hand. the wizard summoned an elemental spell of chain lightning passing through Mayflower and striking Shadow. As Mayflower cried out in pain, Shadow was thrown back 10 feet. His side was smoking from the blast. He laid there, recovering from this attack while the wizard cut his hand conjuring up a vicious blood demon with sharp claws to tear them apart.

Mayflower recovered first. Seeing the blood demon, she waved her arm and mumbled the same words that she read earlier. The blood demon began to shake, then his body exploded, spraying blood everywhere. Mayflower said, "Yesss! I got the spell right."

She clapped her hands and jumped up and down with joy. The wizard's eyes grew wide as he watched this happen. This gave Shadow time to recover, so he could cast a purify spell on the wizard. As he screamed in pain, his flesh slowly began to turn into stone. Within seconds, his body was solid. Mayflower cast a shatter spell that blew the wizard all to pieces. After this, the group gathered together and looked at the crystal ball.

Grunch said, "This is pure evil. It must be destroyed."

Mayflower reached down to pick it up, saying, "I'll destroy it."

Grunch said, "No stop! You have no idea of what you are doing. I'll destroy it while you wait here."

Mayflower said, "I want to go and see how you destroy this."

Grunch said, "I cannot take you along; you would not survive the blast.

You may watch from there," and he pointed to the highest part of the run-down castle. They both vanished with the crystal ball.

Mayflower appeared on top of the castle while Grunch appeared a mile away in an open field filled with zombies. Grunch dropped the crystal ball as his war hammer appeared in his hand. With one mighty swing, he shattered the orb, creating a very large explosion that made a crator 60-feet wide and 20-feet deep around himself. It sent many zombies flying into the air, even from a mile away!

The blast could be felt as body parts rained down onto the group. A hand landed on Mayflower's head with its fingers trying to get a grip. She brushed it off and asked, "Does anyone need a hand?"

As it slowly moved away, an upper torso landed by Night Crawler and started crawling toward her. She said, with excitement, "Ah yum, food that comes to me!"

Grunch reappeared with burn marks on his arm and his war hammer. As he wiped them clean. Night Crawler crawled over to the group and said, "How can I eat the dead one? He is full of deadly blades." Grunch snapped his finger, and the deadly blades disappeared. Night Crawler went to the corpse and asked, "Would anyone like to join me in this good feast?"

The Minotaur was leaning against a broken wall munching on a hand with wiggling fingers. He got up and walked over and cut off a leg with his battle axe and began to enjoy his meal. Night Crawler was very pleased not to be eating alone.

Grunch turned to Mayflower and said, "That wizard had a ring of protection I took from him. You did well in that battle, and you deserve this." He placed the ring on her finger. It resized itself to fit her perfectly.

Mayflower could feel the power in the ring flowing throughout her body. She said, "Thank you for such a beautiful gift."

They got their things together and started traveling once again. By sundown, they came upon an old farm, and the farmer came out to greet them, saying, "You may stay the night if you can help me with some chores."

The group was tired and agreed to help in the morning.

As they all went to the barn for the night. The farmer said, "I hope your pet spider won't eat any of my livestock."

Grunch said, "You have nothing to worry about."

During the night there was an attack by a group of four ghouls with sharp teeth and claws, looking for food. The farmer woke up in alarm, and Stew charged the first ghoul but missed the filthy creature. The ghoul brought down his sharp claws, ripping open the back of the minotaur, blood began to pour out onto the ground. Grunch stepped forward with his war hammer in hand, and with one mighty swing, he crushed the foul creature's head, killing it instantly. Big Red ran into the fight, swinging his claymore and cutting one ghoul in half. Shadow was at his side and blew fire onto another, killing it. Mayflower cast an exploding flesh spell that blew the last one to pieces as flesh and blood sprayed everywhere. She said, "Ah, I didn't know that one was so strong."

In the morning, the farmer said, "I must remove a stump."

Grunch said, "Let's make a bet, if I can pull out your stump, you will sell me a cart and an ox. If I cannot, then I will pay 500,000 in gold pieces."

The farmer smiled because the stump was 15 feet around, and he thought, *No man or a team of oxen can do this.* Grunch saw a brush pile off to one side a hundred yards away. He went to the stump as his friends watched. He griped it with both hands. His powerful muscles began to flex as veins started to pop out. The earth under his feet sank from the weight of ripping out the old stump. He threw it into the brush pile.

The farmer and his wife watched in disbelief from their porch. They could not believe what they just saw! Grunch walked over to them and handed the farmer a bag of gems. The farmer's wife asked, "Who are you people? I've never seen such strength."

Big Red got the war horses, ox, and cart ready to travel as Grunch said, "I am Grunch, and these are my friends."

Stew and Night Crawler left the barn and approached Grunch. Night Crawler said good morning to the farmer's wife. The lady was surprised to see a seven-foot-tall spider that could talk. Grunch shook their hands and said, "Thank you for your kindness. I'm going to leave you with a gift. A powerful staff of protection, so you won't have to worry about evil creatures anymore."

He climbed onto the back of Night Crawler. As the others got ready for traveling, rain began to pour down. Mayflower said, "It's about time you all get clean."

They traveled in the rain until sunset. When the rain stopped, they found themselves near a graveyard. Grunch asked, "Do we keep going or rest for the night?"

They decided to push forward. Big Red said, "I have a weird feeling about this place."

As they entered the graveyard, they could see ghosts milling about. As they neared the center of the graveyard, a ghost of a little girl appeared, sitting next to Big Red on the cart. She said, "Hello—would you like to play a game with me?" She turned her head and saw a ghoul sitting on a tombstone, eating a human hand. She got frightened and vanished. The ghoul spotted them and cried out in alarm.

A voice said, "This is going to be trouble!"

From out of nowhere, ghouls attacked from every direction before anyone could react. Ghouls jumped on Big Red and started biting and clawing him, ripping his flesh from his body as blood gushed from the attacks. He cried out in pain as they began to devour him. Stew jumped off his war horse with his battle axe to help, but it was too late. He was chopping down body after body as blood and body parts covered the ground. Grunch was by his friend's side, swinging his war hammer with one hand and crushing the foul creatures one after another. The ghouls smashed against tombstones and laid still, while, with his other hand, Grunch was grabbing and throwing them, breaking their bodies against other tombstones.

Shadow sprayed a line of fire from his mouth, hitting a dozen ghouls and killing them, then using his claws, he killed six more. Light Foot called out to Shadow, "Get us to safety!"

Shadow was busy fighting and never heard what she had said. He swiped at two ghouls with his claws, disemboweling them. Mayflower was busy on his back. She summoned a ray of starlight to clear a path for their exit. As the star light shot from her hand, It ripped flesh from the ghouls' bodies. Mayflower asked Shadow, "Please RUN!"

Shadow took off. Stew and Grunch stayed behind to battle. Stew fought with all his might but was soon overrun by the bloodthirsty creatures. As they ripped him open and started eating him alive, Grunch was the last man standing, fighting furiously.

He, too, was soon over run as they piled on top of him, clawing and biting at his hands and face. The right side of his face was torn off with blood spraying out. Another ghoul bit down on his wrist, taking off his hand. As more blood sprayed his arm onto the ground, he summoned his inner powers and stood up. bursting with an explosion of pure energy. The blast sent ghouls flying in all directions, killing most. Their bodies rained down, breaking over tombstones as a powerful shock wave spread out stunning the other ghouls and zombies that were remaining.

Grunch went to Night Crawler when she stomped on another ghoul's head even though she was in great pain from having two limbs ripped from her body. Grunch said, "You have a family to care for. I'll send you home now."

As she said, "Thank you," he snapped his fingers on his good hand, and she began to heal. As she vanished, he turned and began walking out of the graveyard. A ghoul charged at him, but he stepped to one side and raised one arm, hitting the foul creature and removing his head. He stopped to take a break.

As his battle wounds began to regenerate and heal in time, the ghost of the little girl appeared sitting next to him and said, "Hello, saw what you did, who are you?"

He said, "My name is Grunch."

She said, "No silly, no man can do what you did."

Grunch replied, "I'm no man, I am a god."

She said, "Well, thank you anyway," and let out a giggle. Grunch let out a laugh and asked her if she would like to leave this evil place and live in a place of peace. She said, "Yes, I sure would, but can my mommy come, too?"

He said, "Of course."

Her mother appeared next to her; she was a beautiful young woman when she died. She said, "Thank you," as they both disappeared.

Grunch decided it was time to get moving. As he got up, he heard a bark coming from behind him. He looked back to see a ghost of a small puppy. Grunch whistled, and it came running over and tried to lick him. He read on the dog tag, her name was doggy. She got really excited and began barking and running in circles around them. Grunch looked on around and then up to see a giant eagle preparing to land with a black headed figure on its back. The eagle landed a short distance away. Grunch walked over and recognized who the rider was.

"How are you, Kran?"

Kran said, "Your ghost dog is very loud."

Grunch turned to doggy and said, "Thank you for your warning, I'll give you a good home."

Grunch snapped his fingers, and the dog disappeared. Kran said, "Do you need a ride?"

Grunch said, "Yes, let's go."

They both climbed on the back of the large eagle and took flight.

"Where's Shadow?" Kran asked.

Grunch replied, "We should see him in a little bit."

Kran let Grunch know that a war between wizards was on its way.

Meanwhile, Shadow ran through the forest that was beyond the graveyard with Mayflower and Light Foot still on his back. Suddenly, Shadow skidded to a stop at the edge of a 1,500-foot cliff that overlooked a very tall, dark tower surrounded by a hundred-feet of pure black sand. He told them, "We are going down."

As he started down the side of the cliff, Light Foot let out a terrified scream and yelled, "You are going to kill us all, you big, dumb beast!" At that moment, he leaped from the wall as she said, "We are going to die! We're going to die, and it's all your fault! You big, dumb animal!" Then they vanished.

When they reappeared, the black sand was only a short distance away. Before Shadow could take a step, a sand lizard ran out and disintegrated before their eyes.

Light Foot jumped off and walked around to face Shadow. She pointed her finger at him and said, "Don't ever do that again!"

As she gently scratched between his eyes, Mayflower said, "I'm hungry..."

Light Foot asked, "How can you possibly be hungry after that?"

Mayflower said, "Ah, he loves to do that. He's not a normal cat. Let's stop and rest a while."

A short time later, a large shadow passed over them, and they all looked up to see a very large eagle circling around them. They scattered for cover as the large eagle gently landed near their fire.

Grunch and Kran climbed off the large eagle. Shadow saw who had arrived. He got excited, ran, and pounced on Kran as Kran said, "I've missed you, too."

Mayflower and Light Foot looked at each other, not knowing what to say. Mayflower asked Grunch, "Who is this person? And where is Big Red and Stew?"

"They didn't make it. This is an old friend who is a very powerful wizard, his name is Kron."

As they all were sitting around the fire, Kran reached into the fire and pulled out an ember to light his pipe. Mayflower noticed that his hands had no flesh on them, and the ember did not burn him. He said, "I must go now. I have much to tend to."

While he was talking, Mayflower and Light Foot walked over to pet the magnificent eagle. As they both said, "Pretty bird."

Kran looked at them and said, "Mayflower, I'll teach you more spells another day." He mounted the giant eagle and took flight.

Early in the morning before the sun rose, Grunch walked onto the black sand. He could sense thousands of dead souls in this sand. He fell to his knees with tears rolling down his face as he recognized some of these souls were his missing friends within moments.

The genie Efreeti appeared. This 10-foot giant said, "I shall destroy you as well."

This woke up Shadow and the others. Grunch asked Mayflower and Shadow, "Would either one of you two like to fight this one?"

As he laughed, Mayflower said, "Really, you've gotta be joking. I'll pass. This one is all yours."

Grunch told Mayflower, "Don't worry, I've got this one. You and Light Foot go to that tower. It's in there, you will need Light Foot to get you to the top."

Mayflower could see a platform just outside of a strong wooden door. She turned to Shadow and said, "It's not big enough for all of us."

Shadow said, "I must go home now," then vanished into this air.

Mayflower placed a hand on Light Foot and teleported them to the platform. Light Foot went to work picking the lock on the door!

Grunch gripped his war hammer, and he and Efreeti charged towards each other, colliding with a great force. Grunch's first blow nailed Efreeti on his side, breaking some of his armor while Efreeti's blade of fire struck Grunch across the chest, and pieces of armor flew off from the powerful blow. Grunch and Efreeti struck out at each other once again. As they continued to do this, Grunch got lucky and shattered Efreeti's wooden shield that he was using. Efieeti brought down his sword once again, slashing Grunch across the chest and opening a large gash with blood pouring out. Grunch swung his war hammer with great force, nailing Efreeti chest and breaking off part of his armor.

Once again, they charged at each other, making contact. As bones in Efreet's right leg shattered by the blow from Grunch's hit. Efreeti's sword came down deep inside Grunch's right shoulder, pouring out blood once again onto the battlefield. They both step back to heal themselves. Efreeti asked, "Who are you?"

"I'm the dwarf who is going to destroy you!"

As they collided once again, Efreeti's blade struck Grunch's left shoulder, cutting very deep and spilling blood onto the sand as they continued to battle.

Mayflower watched from the platform. Light Foot pulled her through the open door and closed it behind them. They made their way up the stairs with Light Foot disarming trap after trap.

Efreeti struck Grunch, bringing his great blade down across his entire body with blood spraying in all directions. Grunch summoned his inner strength and hit Efretti in the chest, shattering his war hammer and sending Efreeti back 20 feet. Efretti's armor started rebuilding itself as Grunch watched in amazement. Grunch took the time to heal most of his battle wounds as his great battle axe reappeared in his hands. Efretti noticed this weapon appeared in Grunch's hands, and they both stepped forward swinging at each other, Efreeti's blade sunk deep in to Grunch's right side, spraying blood everywhere. Grunch's great battle ax removed Efreeti's right arm at the elbow, and blood sprayed out as Efteeti's arm fell onto the sand.

Grunch struck again, wedging his great battle axe deep inside Efreeti's chest. As blood poured out, he yelled in great pain. Efreeti brought down his weapon again, burying it deep inside Grunch's right shoulder. He staggered back a few steps and fell to his knees as Efrettis' sword struck Grunch in the chest, impaling him. Efreeti put his foot on Grunch's chest and pulled his blade free. As he ripped the great sword from his chest, Efrettis threw it down in disgust next to Grunch's limp body with blood pooling around him. Efretti then vanished to heal his wounds.

There was a sound of trees snapping as a huge giant made her way through the forest. She stopped at the edge of the black sand, knelt down, and picked up Grunch. As she held Grunch in her hands, her body began to glow. Then she pulled some moss from her body and gently covered him with it. Her glow faded for a moment as he began to heal.

Grunch knelt down on one knee in her hand and said, "Thank you, my fair lady. I can't believe it; I know who you are, but I've only heard myths about you."

She gently set him down and took a step back. She sat down to watch the rest of his fight. She wanted to see who was able to do this to a god.

As he turned to face the sand, Grunch summoned his shadow demon dragon hide armor with one of the last swords. The huge woman said, "My god, the swords do exist! They are as beautiful as they are powerful."

Grunch stepped back onto the black sand. Efreeeti once again appeared and said, "You again? I thought I killed you!"

He noticed the armor and then the very dangerous sword and his eyes grew wider with hate and fear.

They charged once again. Efreeti struck Grunch across the chest, but this time it left no marks on his battle armor. As Grunch laughed, his sword sliced through Efreeti's sword like butter. Grunch again struck out at him, cutting open his armor and into his great chest with ease spilling out a massive amount of blood with guts. With one final, mighty blow, he slashed upward, slicing Efreeti in two.

Light Foot and Mayflower made it to the top of the stairs, Light Foot picked the lock. As she heard a click, she stepped back, letting Mayflower open the door. In the middle of this big room was the dark crystal. Standing in front of it was a powerful lady with blue skin, deep blue eyes, and black hair. She wore a black gem around her neck that was glowing. Mayflower asked, "Who are you?"

"I'm Marid, I'm here to—" Without any warning, Mayflower cast a spell to remove the glowing gem from around Marid's neck. The instant it was removed, Marid said, "Thank you for removing that cursed item from me. I will grant you one wish."

Mayflower pulled out the piece of crystal and handed it to Marid. Marid found where the piece fit. She put it right in place. Suddenly, it began to hum, and she turned to Mayflower and Light Foot and said, "Let us leave now!"

Mayflower said, "I wish you would come and live with us," as they all vanished, reappearing at the edge of the sand in front of Grunch. As the crystal exploded with such force it destroyed the tower, leaving only a big crater behind, Grunch said, "I am proud of you two. Now it is time to go home."

Mayflower told Grunch, "We have another guest. Her name is Marid, and she needs a home."

Grunch said, "Very well." Then, he turned and said, "Thank you for helping me."

The giant woman was still sitting there. She got up and said, "I must go now. Others are in need of me."

As she vanished into the forest, Grunch transported them all back to his great hall. He said, "It's time for a great feast to celebrate our victory." The hall was then filled with tables of food. He said, "I have one other matter to attend to," and vanished.

He appeared at the front door of John and Tina's home. He knocked, and a soft voice said, "Please come in."

He stepped inside and noticed John was not at home. The children came running, and each gave Grunch a hug. Tina said, "John is out earning money."

Grunch snapped his fingers, and John appeared with a drumstick in his mouth and a mug of beer in his hand. Tina grew angry and said, "Is this what you call 'earning money'?"

The girls brought out Little Thief, saying, "It was a lot of fun to watch over him. He kept bringing us shinny things."

Grunch said, "I am in need of you and your family's help. Big Red has been killed, and someone needs to watch over the treasure and the last swords. Your family would have to move, but I will prepare everything for your arrival."

Tina jumped up in excitement and asked, "We would be living in the cave we visited?"

Grunch said, "Yes," as John said, "I don't want to go live in a cave." Grunch snapped his fingers and took John to the cave. He showed him the treasure rooms and the last swords; they discussed how the cave would be fixed up as Grunch put away his demon slayer sword.

When they reappeared back at John's home, his attitude was changed. They both were excited and wanted to know when it would be ready for them to live in. Grunch said, "It is ready now."

They packed their belongings, and Grunch transported them all to their new home. He picked up Little Thief and handed him to the girls and said, "This is his home, too, watch after my friend." He turned to John and Tina and said, "This mirror works as a two-way mirror. You can come and visit me anytime. Now, there's a celebration I must get back to. You are welcome to come along if you wish."

In the great hall, a celebration was taking place with Mayflower, Shadow, and Light Foot. When Grunch and John's family showed up, he noticed not everyone was there. He clapped his hands, and the twins appeared, covered in jewels and sleeping soundly. He let the little girls wake them up with Little Thief. He snapped his fingers, and Night Crawler arrived. She was completely healed and was glad to be back home. The ghost of a little girl appeared with her mommy next to him and said, "Hello, would you like to play a game with me?"

Grunch played with her for a little bit, then the little girl got up and ran to a little puppy saying, "Oh doggy, I thought I'd never see you again."

She approached Grunch in tears and thanked him for doing what no one else could. He found her lost puppy.

The rest of the night was a pleasant celebration.

3

RESCUE

Mayflower was not feeling very well. She left the party to get some rest. During the night, while she slept, she floated out of her body and traveled to her village. She witnessed her people being slaughtered by shadow demons. Bodies littered the ground as they killed everyone that stood in their way. One demon noticed Mayflower and struck out at her, slashing her across the chest, spilling blood onto the ground where she stood. She screamed out in pain and woke up in her bed, covered in blood. As she removed the bloody clothing, she saw five gashes across her chest. She cast a spell of mass healing on herself. Within moments, the deep gashes disappeared. It didn't take long to clean the bloody mess.

Mayflower knew that she had to go home. She wondered if she should have someone go with her but decided not to. She spent the day preparing for her journey. She left at sunset.

As she teleported herself off the island, she missed the shore by 12 feet and ended up chest deep in water. She walked onto the shore, feeling wet and foolish. She started a warm fire and hung her wet cloths to dry and fell asleep. The next morning, when she woke up, a lady was sitting by the fire looking at her.

Mayflower asked, "Who are you?"

The reply was, "My name is Lulu. I'm cold and hungry, please help me?"

Mayflower decided to cook a good meal for the both of them. She asked Lulu, "Why are you so beautiful?"

"I'm one of the thunder mountains, as is Mars. Thank you again for the good meal."

A troupe of orcs emerged from the woods with battle axes in their hands charging them both.

Mayflower and Lulu both cast spells together, striking the orcs with exploding darts and magic missiles and causing flesh and blood to fly in all directions as their bodies crumpled to the ground. Mayflower looked at Luna and said, "Good job, girl."

Lulu said, "These woods are not safe, would you like some company?"

Mayflower answered, "Yes, I would like your company."

After a few days of travel, they reached Mayflower's village. As they entered the village, they saw bodies of men, women, and children lying everywhere. The carnage was total. Blood pooled on the ground around the dead. They heard a growling noise and looked in that direction. They spotted a shadow demon dragging a man by his hair on the ground. The demon stopped and looked at them both as he picked up the man and ripped out his throat with blood spraying everywhere.

Soon, there were hundreds of them. Mayflower and Lulu were striking down demon after demon with their spells but were overwhelmed. They were bound and taken to a large cave where a few other women were in cages. Mayflower began to talk with them.

A man appeared in front of Mayflower and Lulu, looking them both over, then he went to speak with the leader of the shadow demons. A deal was made and a pack of 12 werewolves took all of the women and bound them together in a line with chains and shackles.

As they marched through the deep forest, Mayflower told Lulu, "I think they have plans for us."

Suddenly, they were attacked by a band of bugbears. The werewolves never stood a chance. The bugbears swung their morning stars with mighty death blows, crushing the heads of four werewolves. Their bodies laid on the ground with pools of blood around them and bits of flesh ripped from their faces. Another bugbear sunk his morning star deep into the chest of another werewolf, causing bits of flesh and blood to spray out onto the ground. Five of the remaining werewolves started running away. One was struck with a javelin, killing him on the spot. The bugbears continued marching the prisoners throughout the night.

In the morning, Mayflower and Lulu saw a demon appear and told the bugbears that the pit fiend would pay for Mayflower and Lulu.

As the others were set free, Grunch was sitting in his throne room addressing his knights. He was angry for letting their king be assassinated by a paid killer. Kran appeared at Grunch's front door at the same time as a little demon appeared. Kran asked, "What brings you here?"

"I bring a personal message for Grunch only."

They entered the castle together and went to the throne room. When they opened the doors, sitting on a perch was a phoenix, saying, "Be careful, you dumb dwarf, that's a stupid demon."

There were 50 knights sitting around his tables, and Grunch sat on this throne.

Grunch said, "Kran, why did you bring this foul demon into my home?"

The little demon said, "I bring you a message."

Grunch stood up and said, "First I have business to deal with. For your failure, there will be a battle between all of you, and there can only be one winner. The battle will begin…now."

Grunch sat down to enjoy his meal.

The knights jumped to their feet, drawing their weapons and started slaughtering each other. Within moments, half of them laid on the floor covered in blood. Five more had their heads removed as blood sprayed into the air.

One knight caught Grunch's full attention, this knight used two short swords. Every move he made was as deadly as his last. With great speed, he buried his sword deep into the chest of the knights, pulling them free as he turned quickly and sliced another across the belly, letting guts and blood fall to the floor. As he fell backwards, more blood sprayed everywhere. Grunch recognized this fighting style and grinned to himself. There were only two left standing in pools of blood and body parts.

Grunch said, "Continue the fight," as the two face each other.

The knight that Grunch was watching threw down both of his bloody, short swords and said, "I don't need these to kill you."

The other knight charged at him and missed with his sword. He grabbed the knight by his head and snapped his neck as his body fell to the floor. Grunch said, "You fight well. I have seen your style of fighting before. Now sit and enjoy a meal. We will talk more later. Now, you little demon, what is this about a message for me, you foul creature?"

The little demon handed him a scroll and said, "You're the foul one, you stupid dwarf," then vanished. The message read:

After reading the letter, Grunch set down his goblet, he didn't notice it was crushed by his hand. Grunch told Kean they were going to need some help. He snapped his fingers, and the room was clean. Shadow and Marid appeared. Shadow knew something was about to happen, so he sat next to the fighter, staring at him as he ate. Kran spoke up, saying, "I came here to teach Mayflower more magic. Where is she, Grunch?"

Grunch read the message again out loud for them all to hear.

Kran said, "This sounds like a rescue that will take all of us. Let's go now."

Grunch said, "Not yet," he snapped his fingers, and a human lich appeared.

This living corpse with blue glowing eyes asked, "Why have I been summoned here Grunch?"

Grunch said, "You are needed for a special quest."

"Very well then, I'll go and help you."

Grunch told the group, "I shall return shortly," then he vanished.

He reappeared knee deep in the city fountain. A little girl said, "Silly old man, you're going to get into trouble if you play in that fountain."

A few Knights of the Blue Rose said, "Hey you! Come out of there."

They arrested him and took him to jail. He had to sit for a few hours for his minor infraction. Grunch sat on the bed and asked, "When's lunch?" He turned to see a guard bringing Tina in. She said, "He is a good friend. Can I stay and visit with him?"

One of the guards said that would be fine.

Grunch said, "Can you please help me? I need a weapon from the holy room, can you please recover it for me?"

She asked, "Where is the holy room?"

"I will guide you to a certain chest. When you open the chest, you will find some stairs going down about 300 feet. At the bottom, you will find a short hallway. At the end of the hall, there will be beautiful golden door.

Inside that room is the weapon I need." He reached up and plucked out one of his eyes and gently wrapped it into a blue cloth and handed it to her. "This will guide you to the weapon I need."

Tina asked, "Didn't that hurt?"

"Not as much as you would think," he said as he smiled at her.

The guard came by and said, "Time to go, young lady."

After she left, the guards released a very large barbarian. He stopped at Grunch's cell and said, "You stupid dwarf, I hate people like you. If you got a problem with that, you ugly, stinking bag of meat, meet me at Two Fingers Tavern. There's a fighting pit we can use. They know me very well; I have never been beat."

As the guards had been trying to get him to move. He laughed as he said, "I'll see you soon, stupid dwarf," he said as he spit on Grunch and walked out.

As Tina was walking home, she was thinking, *What chest? He's got so many; will I have to open them all?* She started getting excited to see some holy weapons and armor and started walking faster. When she arrived back home, she went straight to the room that was filled with many chests. She unwrapped his eye. It began to move within her hand. Within minutes, it showed her, which chest to open. She got excited again and let out a squeal as she opened the chest and found some stairs going down. She climbed into the chest and went down the stairs.

When she reached the bottom, she found a beautiful golden door at the end of a short hallway. She entered the chamber and was surprised to see how many weapons and armor there were. She got really excited when she saw Excalibur stuck in the stone along with all the beautiful holy weapons and armor. She pulled out his eye once again and asked, "Which one?" It looked towards a very beautiful long silver sword.

The guard told Grunch, "Your time is up, you can go."

Grunch walked out and asked the first person he saw, "Where is Two Fingers Tavern?" After getting directions he went on his way.

As he passed an alley, he heard a cry for help. Four men were robbing a beautiful woman. He went to help her. As he approached them, they attacked him with short swords. One of them sliced his chest open, spilling blood onto the ground. Grunch just laughed about it. The woman was frozen in place as she watched what just happened.

One of them said, "Stay out of this, or we will kill you."

Grunch stepped beck and raised his hand. A double-bladed battle axe appeared in it. Without a warning, he stepped right into them as he was swinging his weapon, cutting open one of them across his belly, spilling blood and guts to the ground. He turned, swinging his weapon once again and sinking it deep into the chest of one of the others, causing a massive amount of blood to spray all over himself. The other two watched in horror as he used his foot to free his weapon as the body fell to the ground. He turned towards the other two as they ran away gripped in fear. The woman tried to thank him, but he just turned and walked away as his weapon vanished.

He found the tavern and walked in. There was a crowd of people with fighters present, and he was able to find the barbarian easily. His loud and obnoxious voice could be heard above the crowd. He approached the barbarian and said, "Hey you! Let's fight."

They both jumped into the bloody pit. The barbarian had his great long sword; Grunch didn't have a weapon. The barbarian asked, "Are you that stupid? You dumb dwarf, where's your weapon?"

"I don't need a weapon to teach you a lesson."

The barbarian noticed the deep slice across Grunch's chest and said, "It looks as if someone has already started with you. I will finish the job. Prepare to die!" The barbarian swung his great sword.

Grunch caught the barbarian's weapon with his bare hands, snapping the blade like a twig. Before the barbarian could do anything, Grunch grabbed him by the arm and pulled him near and said, "Do you know who I am? I'm the god of rampage."

The barbarian's eyes grew wide. With brute force, Grunch kicked him. As the barbarian flew across the pit and into the wall, Grunch still a hold of his arm, the barbarian cried out in pain as his blood covered the ground. The tavern grew silent. The woman from the alley yelled, "Kill the bastard! He killed my husband."

Grunch walked over to the barbarian and grabbed his good arm and tossed him up out of the pit. He landed in front of the woman as a long knife appeared in her hand. She plunged it into his chest. Grunch stood there and laughed as blood began to run out. Grunch jumped out of the 10-foot pit and said, "I need a beer."

As the knife vanished, the woman said, "I'll buy you that beer. Please come and drink with me, so we can talk." The woman said, "My name is

Mary, and before you disappear again, I need to say thank you for helping me earlier."

Just then bartender came over and said, "Your bill has been taken care of. Can I bring you something to eat?"

"Mary can order for me."

She ordered two mugs of milk and two steak dinners. After their meal, she asked, "Will you walk me home?"

Grunch answered, "It would be my honor."

Twenty minutes, later they came to an ordinary looking house. Mary asked him, "Would you come in and sit and talk with me for a while?"

They talked into the night. Mary grew tired and offered him the spare room.

The next morning, he awoke early and left before Mary woke up. He left behind a bag of blue gems and a thank you note.

He enjoyed the morning air as he walked to John and Tina's house.

Tina saw him coming. She grabbed the sword and ran out to meet him. He asked, "May I have my eye please?"

Tina pulled out the eye wrapped in cloth and handed it to him. As he put it back in place, she noticed a slice across his chest and asked, "Does that hurt?"

"I'm used to injuries. You did well in finding the weapon I need."

She giggled when she said, "I had no idea all that was there. I told no one of your treasures."

He took his holy sword and appeared back in his throne room. He called everyone together as they sat and had a meal. During the meal, the Morlock showed up at his front door. Grunch snapped his fingers to bring the creature to the throne room and said, "What is your name?"

"My name is Rath. I've been instructed to show you to the underworld but not to interfere. We will leave when you are ready."

Grunch said, "Let's go."

He led them all to a two-way dimensional mirror then stepped through and waited for the others to arrive. When they all showed up, Rath stepped forward and said, "I brought these three people, so let us pass, you two overgrown guard dummies."

The 15-foot-tall gate keepers opened the gates to the underworld.

As they walked, they heard a deep growling. Out of nowhere a pack of hellhounds attacked them before they could even draw their weapons. One bit Grunch on the arm and tried to breathe fire, which did no good. He was able to pry open its mouth, splitting its jaw in two and sinking its sharp teeth deep into Neraph's rotten flesh. He placed his hand on the hound's head and set off a scorching ray spell, exploding the head. The last one grabbed Kran by the leg and started shaking violently as Kran was able to cast a spell to blast its body apart, leaving only its head attached to his leg. The floor was covered with blood and guts from his spell.

Grunch said, "I think your spell was a little too strong!" as all three laughed.

They continued down the path. They had to clear away grown vines that hung from the ceiling until they reached a fork in the path. Kran said, "It's this way," as he went to the right around some steam vents. They followed the path to a wooden door.

Rath said, "You stupid people, you took the wrong one," as he opened the door violently, which knocked into a nest of spiders that rained down into the group. The group was angry and Rath said, "Remember, you can't harm me." They saw a room full of green and brown fungus along with huge stalactite hung of the roof. There were also pots of boiling water with small creatures crawling everywhere. Off in one corner hung from the ceiling were body parts.

As they were looking, a large demon was pushing a big wooden cart full of body parts. He stopped and pulled a giant meat cleaver from the cart. Grunch, Kran, and Neraph drew their weapons. The demon charged towards them as they all collided with each other at the same time. The demon got lucky, hitting Grunch in the shoulder. As a mist of blood sprayed up into the air, Kran sliced the demon across the back, and within seconds, he was healed. The demon pulled his cleaver free from Grunch's shoulder and turned, quickly sinking his bloody weapon deep into Kran's shoulder as blood sprayed outwards onto the floor. Neraph cast a spell, sending a wave of magic missiles, striking the demon in the chest. Chunks of flesh and blood flew in every direction. The demon got angry and grabbed Kran by the throat, then slammed him into the ground as his bloody body went limp. Grunch took his holy sword swinging his weapon downwards severing the demons head from his body as his body dropped onto the floor with a pool of blood around it. The room was clear and opened up to a path on the other side.

Grunch took the time to heal Kran and himself. They decided to rest and have a good meal before going on.

They followed the vines and roots on the cave floor going downwards. Soon, they came to the edge of a huge lake. They noticed large steam vents along with huge stalagmites sticking out of the lake and stalactites hung from the ceiling. They turned and noticed a barge with a ferryman that had a head of a goat with a body of a human waiting for his passengers. They boarded the barge and sat while the ferryman held out a hand for payment. Grunch put a red gem into his hand. As he closed his hand, the gem vanished.

They began to cross the lake. Grunch looked into the lake and faces of lost souls. The trip across the lake was filled with dangers as swarms of fire bats overhead dipped down trying to take bits out of them. They made it to the other side and continued their quest.

From out of the darkness emerged some creatures that stood four feet tall with rows of sharp teeth and claws. They started attacking the group. Neraph was bitten on the leg, and Grunch was bitten on the arm. As both of them were paralyzed, Kran cast a protection spell from evil that caused the creatures to go back into the darkness from where they came. Kran cast a healing spell over them all. Within minutes, they were all healed.

Rath said, "Let's go, it's this way." He led them to another door. They opened the door and went down the stairs. At the bottom, there were green vines hung from the ceiling with a hall littered with beetles and centipedes and bones.

Grunch told the group, "Prepare for anything."

As they went down the hall, stepping on the remains of those who died here, Rath said, "I've never been this way before. They came to a set of bars blocking their way to a stone door."

Grunch grabbed the bars and ripped them free, then ran and crashed through the stone door. In the center of the room was a floating cube. Rath reached out for it, but it was an illusion. Suddenly, a portal was opened, and a chain demon stepped through. He said, "I will tear your flesh apart!"

Chains appeared from nowhere, hooking onto Grunch, Kran, and Neraph in several areas, and pulled flesh from their bones as blood covered the floor. Suddenly, Grunch got hooked again with two chains in the back that pierced through his body, pulling him backwards. He grabbed the chains and pulled them through his body as he grunted in pain. Neraph opened up the palm of his hand and cast a scorching ray hitting the demon right in the chest, sending chunks of flesh flying out from his body.

Seconds later, Kran struck him with six magic missiles, blasting more chunks of flesh into the air. The chain demon roared in frustration; he had never before encountered anyone like this.

As he watched in horror, Rath crept up behind him and swung a short sword, slicing off the chain demon's head. He said, "See, I can kill also, you stupid people."

Grunch said, "Let's get moving," as he was healing the group.

On the side of the room, there was an opening that led to another hallway. This one was covered in moss and had green slime dripping from the ceiling and running down the sides of the walls. Grunch held out his hand and a drop of slime landed on it. Grunch pulled back his hand quickly. There was a hole through his flesh. Rath took three steps into the hallway, and spikes shot up from floor to ceiling, impaling Rath through his body in many places. Grunch needed to think of what he would need to do. Kran leaned against the wall and fell through into another hallway that led around the slime and moss.

They soon entered a very large and deep cavern with large stalactite hung from the ceiling. The path turned into a stone bridge that led 550 feet across the cavern but was only wide enough for one person, so they formed a line with Grunch in front and Kran in the rear. Halfway across the bridge, a mist appeared. As they entered the mist, they found themselves back at the start of the bridge. The second time crossing the bridge, Grunch cast a wind spell that blew the mist from their path. At the far end, a fireball hit Grunch in the chest, knocking him back into Neraph. In front of them were eight six-foot-tall fire frogs spitting fireballs at them. The next fireball came at Grunch, and he batted it away with his hand. Kran and Neraph's fire magic missiles hit two fire frogs, which exploded on impact. One leaped to close to the edge and fell over, plunging to its death below. After seeing the success from the magic missiles, Kran and Neraph started casting more fatal strikes. The large frogs exploded one after the other, spraying the area beyond them with blood and guts.

At the exit of the large cavern stood a gate made of iron flanked by 30-foot stone structurers. Grunch said, "Looks like we're supposed to go this way." Soon, they ran into a death knight who had his blade out and ready to fight. Grunch said, "This shouldn't take long, you both stay back."

As Grunch pulled out his holy sword, they both collided with each other. They connected with a terrible sound of steel on steel. The death knight swung, again slicing Grunch across his right shoulder. As blood ran down his arm, Grunch swung his holy sword, hitting the death knight in the leg and causing a gash to open up. They once again continued blocking and clashing with each other. Finally, they both stepped back from each other. Kran stepped forward, swinging his sword, and the death knight was swinging as well with another terrible sound. Kran's sword was cut in two. Grunch brought up his sword, blocking the death knight's blade from hitting Kran. Neraph was casting spells that had no effect on him. Grunch said, "I guess we're going to have to do this the hard way," as his god slayer sword appeared in Grunch's hand. The death knight swung his sword and caught Grunch across the leg, slicing open a very deep gash. Grunch swung his god slayer sword, hitting the death knight, cutting him in half with ease as his body fell to the ground in a pool of blood around it.

After the fight, Grunch healed himself. He spoke to Kran, saying, "I told you to stay back. You are lucky that you only lost your weapon."

Kran said, "I still have my quarter staff."

They continued on their way.

They came to a door made out of human bones. Grunch ran to the door crashing through it and tumbling all the way down the stairs. He just sat there shaking his head feeling foolish. The others caught up and looked around. They were in a room filled with mirrors. In the center of the room was a floating crystal. As Grunch picked himself up from the floor, the images from the mirrors stepped through, prepared to fight. Every move that was made, the images also made; they were evenly matched. Every injury that was given was also received. After what seemed like hours, Grunch said, "Maybe it's this crystal, let's destroy it."

He walked over to the floating gem and told Neraph and Kran to head back upstairs as his war hammer appeared in his hand. He brought down his weapon, shattering the crystal with ease, and the images vanished. The explosion he was expecting never came. He called the others back down. When they arrived, they saw 15 paths. Neraph said, "Let's take the center path."

After walking for an hour, they heard some strange noises, and they stopped. They saw a weird looking creature with a painted face and red nose, with mixed colors of blue, orange, and green hair. He wore large shoes and a clown suit with a fake flower that shot acid from it. Kran told the group, "I know of this clown, he's evil in a very dangerous way."

The clown approached, juggling sharp knives. Without a warning, the knives flew from his hands toward the group. The group was able to jump out of the way but was blasted by exploding rubber chickens. The group lost large chunks of their flesh from the exploding rubber chickens, causing blood to ooze from their wounds. As the clown honked his red nose, he let out an evil laugh. As the group watched him, he reached down and started pulling a thin string which led to a small cannon which fired exploding minions. The group looked at each other as he turned the cannon towards them and fired one at them. It exploded at Neraph's feet taking off his right leg as he fell next to his twitching leg that had pieces of bone and flesh shredded at the knee. He threw another rubber chicken at them, but Kran batted it away. It exploded in Nerpah's face, taking off his head as a mist of blood sprayed up into the air, and his body slumped to the ground. Suddenly, the floor was covered with banana peels.

As they both watched, the clown summoned a cream pie and threw it, hitting Grunch in his face. That angered Grunch. He said, "Oh no, you didn't!" and he started running at the clown, but he slipped and slid down the path. The clown summoned a large rubber mallet, hitting him and sending him back the way he came.

Grunch slammed into Kran, knocking him over as well. The banana peel vanished and the clown said, "Now it's time to get serious." He pulled out an umbrella with a spear tip as he laughed and honked his red nose. He began to stomp his feet, and blades popped out. He started walking toward them both as Grunch and Kran started standing up. Grunch pulled out his god slayer sword and handed Kran his holy sword. The clown stopped 10 feet from them. He opened his umbrella, and tiny darts flew out, hitting both of them. Kran stepped up hitting the clown in the arm and severing it from his body.

Grunch appeared behind the clown and grabbed him, stuffing a rubber chicken into his mouth as the clown's head exploded, covering them both with gore. Kran said, "Really Grunch?"

"He deserved it."

As they took the time to heal themselves then started down a hallway on the other side of the room. At the end of the hall was another door, and they both saw what lay beyond. Four platforms spread 20 feet apart by deep water. On the third platform sat a monk. Kran said, "I think this guy wants to fight." Kran snapped his fingers and reappeared on the same platform with the monk. The monk stood up as Kran pulled out his holy sword. He swung, but the monk was too fast, and Kran missed. The monk jumped up and kicked Kran in the face. Kran swung again at the monk's legs, but the monk jumped over the blade kneed Kran in the chest.

Kran was getting angry as he swung once again. This time, he nicked the monk in the arm, causing a small gash. He started striking Kran with deadly blows. His strikes were too fast for Kran to defend himself. Finally, the monk grabbed hold of him, and together, they both fell into the water. Within seconds, a loud explosion occurred as water mixed with blood and body parts rushed upwards spraying everywhere. Grunch teleported himself across the water and continued on his way.

He came to a four-way split, deciding to take the far-left path. He grinned to himself and out of the darkness Shadow appeared with a drum stick in his mouth. Grunch said, it's you and me old friend, let's go. They continued down the path when they came around a corner and ran into some steel bars. Grunch grabbed the bars and ripen them free with his bare hands.

Within a couple of minutes, they came to a very large cavern with stalactite hung from the ceiling and steam vents. As they were looking around at this large cavern, there were huge boulders and pit of hot lava along with big brown and yellow puff balls everywhere. Suddenly, small needles shot out of nowhere, hitting both of them across the legs causing little spots of blood on them both. Grunch and Shadow looked around and saw some five-foot tall mushrooms. Something caught their eyes. They saw some movement at their right side before they could do anything they were attacked by some small creatures with sharp claws and teeth shredding their flesh. Grunch was able to free his weapon and started killing them one after another, as Shadow was using his nine-inch claws to rip them apart as well. The remaining creatures ran off. Grunch scratched his head and laughed as he healed both of them. Shadow said, "Now what?"

A 30-foot tan cyclops with a huge lava battle axe entered the area. Grunch said, "You had to ask." They looked at each other than charged at the giant.

The giant swung his battle axe, hitting Grunch and sending him flying backwards into some puff balls that exploded. Meanwhile, Shadow struck the huge beast across his legs, causing a very deep gash as the giant growled in pain. With great speed, Shadow sliced through his leg, causing him to fall. When Grunch stood up, he was missing chunks of flesh. As Grunch walked towards the giant, Shadow was bouncing up and down on his back. Grunch buried his sword all the way to the hilt in the giant's head, killing the giant as blood ran out onto the floor. Shadow jumped down and said, "What's next?" then yelled, "Look out!" as Grunch turned just in time as a blade sliced at him. He turned around and stared right into the eyes of a fire demon with a long sword.

Grunch told him, "Just go back to where you came from."

The fire demon turned around and suddenly spun back around, slicing Grunch across his chest with his sword. Grunch grabbed him by his face and power-slammed him into the ground with great force, causing the back of the demon's head to explode as blood and brains sprayed on the ground.

As Shadow said, "You're getting slow in your old age, friend," Grunch started summoning a greater spell that would destroy everything in this room.

They both started down a tunnel when Shadow said, "Hey dummy, aren't you gonna heal yourself as Grunch whispered a healing spell on himself. They both reached another door; this one was guarded by a three-headed devil dog that watched every move they both made. They decided to sit down. Shadow said, "Nice puppy."

Grunch asked, "What's his name?" Unexpectedly the dog went to Grunch's side and laid down. "I'm going to name you Fluffy."

Fluffy wagged his tail.

Shadow said, "Really, are you serious?"

Grunch said, "Let's go."

Grunch opened the door as a blast of hot air hit them. They started going down deeper into the underworld. Fluffy followed behind them. When they reached the bottom, there was a demon with a fire whip and a sword waiting for them. Suddenly, without any warnings, Grunch swung his god slayer sword, decapitating the demon, and his body crumpled to the ground blood pooled all around the lifeless corps. Fluffy grabbed the head on its second bounce and carried away his trophy.

They continued to walk; they came to an open cavern. Sitting on a boulder was a horn demon with his short spear in one hand and in the other was a chain ball. He said, "Let's fight." Before the demon could swing his chain and ball, Fluffy ran up and caught the ball in one of his mouths and began to tug on it as the demon tried to pull free. They both stood there laughing as the demon wrestled with Fluffy.

When the demon raised his short spear, Grunch whistled, and Fluffy let go, wagging his tail. Grunch stepped up to him and swung his first, breaking the demon's jaw. The demon swung his chain and ball, hitting Grunch right in the chest. As the demon plunged his short spear right into Grunch's left shoulder causing blood to spill onto the ground, Grunch stepped back and snapped the handle off of the short spear. As Grunch charged at the demon, grabbing him by his horns and snapped his neck then threw him against the wall.

As this was going on, a tiny demon scurried off to let its master know what just happened. Fluffy chased after the little demon. Grunch and Shadow followed behind. They came to another cavern, and sitting on a bone throne was a 15-foot giant demon with red eyes.

"What is it you both want, Grunch?"

"If you let us pass to continue our journey, I will lay waist to the pit friend demon and then give you his realm."

The demon said, "I will hold you to that deal, Grunch."

As the three of them came to a ledge overlooking a lake of fire, they saw across the lake sat a very huge devil surrounded by lower demons. Shadow and him spotted the two girls in a cage hanging from the ceiling. Shadow and Fluffy watched Grunch walk over to the edge and jump, landing on the cavern's dirt floor with a cloud of dust exploding up around him.

Shadow teleported himself and Fluffy down in to the crowd of lesser demons. Fluffy began to attack three at a time as Shadow blew a cone of fire that vaporized all in its path.

Grunch stepped out with his god slayer sword and started slicing through one body after the next, leaving a trail of blood and dead bodies until they noticed the weapon Grunch was using and scattered, which left him 60 feet away and staring at Asnodeuss.

Meanwhile, Shadow and Fluffy continued to chase down and kill the lesser demon. Without warning, Shadow teleported them both back up to the ledge, so Fluffy could rest.

Asnodeuss stood over 20 feet tall with a wing span in excess of 30 feet and weighed over 2,000 pounds. His thick muscles clung to his gigantic frame and were armored over by dense, bladed scales. He had sharp fangs and claws like daggers. Asnodeuss stood up and said, "You will die today, Grunch."

Grunch was struck by a cone of hellfire and barely survived the attack. Asnodeuss leaped into the air, landing in front of Grunch. Grunch struck out, slicing him in the leg and causing blood to run down. Asnodeuss swung his massive claw at Grunch's head, ripping open a three-inch gash across his face and losing his right eye as blood poured down his face. They both lashed out at the same time. Grunch's blade sliced off a claw as blood sprayed out.

Asnodeuss pulled out a two-handed longsword called Death Blade. Grunch snapped his fingers, and his shadow demon dragon had armor appear on him. They took steps toward each other as their weapons collided, causing sparks to fly from their blades. Asnodeuss was able to land a blow across Grunch's shoulder, slicing through his armor with ease and causing blood to ooze out. He sliced down his arm, then sliced him deep across the belly, and more blood spilled onto the floor.

They traded blows after blows, back and forth. Asnodeuss once again sliced right through Grunch's armor, taking off his left arm as blood sprayed onto the battlefield. Grunch brought his blade upward, striking Asnodeuss in his chest once again and spraying out blood in every direction. Asnodeuss fell to his knees as Grunch plunged his god slayer sword all the way to the hilt in his chest then pulled down to slice open a wound so that his guts spilled out onto the ground.

The giant creature fell over dead in a pool of blood. Grunch picked up the other lost sword and sent it to John and Tina's place along with his god slayer sword, then he looked up and snapped his fingers again as the cage disappeared. Grunch teleported himself back up to the ledge.

Shadow asked, "Do you need a hand old man?"

He told Shadow and Fluffy, "It's time to go home now," as they all vanished. They reappeared in the great hall next to the cage with Mayflower and Lulu. Mayflower said, "Really, you've got to be kidding me, Grunch! Zanlue can you please open the cage, so I can help Grunch out," as Grunch fell over and passed out onto the floor.

The phoenix said, "You stupid dragon, do as you are told."

Zanlue saw Fluffy and turned invisible. Fluffy went to the cage and laid down, looking at the ladies as Marid came walking into the room and saw the cage with Mayflower and Lulu and Grunch on the floor. Grunch was missing an arm and one side of his face was gone. Madrid walked over and opened the cage and then reached down and scratched Fluffy's head, saying, "Good boy."

The three ladies together cast a spell of teleportation on him as he vanished and reappeared in a soft bed. The ladies arrived and started casting full healing while Shadow cast a regeneration spell on him.

A week later, Grunch woke up, hungry and thirsty, so he summoned a meal. He missed Mary, so he teleported himself and reappeared once again back inside the city fountain. The same little girl once again said, "Silly old man." He got out just in time to see Mary sitting by the fountain.

"Hi Mary, do you have some time to visit with me?"

She said, "Yes," and together, they walked to her home.

Grunch asked Mary if she would like to move in with him, she said, "Oh my yes. Will I need much?"

Grunch said, "Take only what you want to keep."

She gathered a few belongings, and together, they vanished. They reappeared in Grunch's castle. Grunch said, There's something I need to tell you. I'm a god." When Mary heard this, she fainted.

She woke up in a very large bed with a very large cat snoring on the floor next to her. Grunch entered and asked if she was feeling better. He told her, "That's Shadow. He is a good friend, and he'll protect you."

As the sun started to set, he pulled a chair to the side and sat down to rest. She asked, "Are you really a god?"

His reply was, "Yes, I really am a god," as she drifted off to sleep once again.

Mary awoke the next morning to find Grunch sitting in his chair and said, "I had a wonderful dream. You were a god…"

Grunch said, "Mary I really am a god, and I would like you to stay with me, but first I must introduce you to everyone who lives here with me."

At this time, Shadow decided to go and visit his friend Mars, so he cast a simple spell and reappeared at the cliff overlooking the small village. As he looked down, he saw an army of orcs and ogres that were killing men, women, and children. He noticed two ogres chasing a little seven-year-old girl into a home.

Shadow teleported himself down to face the ogre. As he appeared, his nine-inch claws were out. He struck the first one with fire from his mouth, killing the creature on the spot. Before the second ogre could react, Shadow attacked him with his claws, tearing the flesh from the ogre's face as he dropped to his knees in pain. Shadow struck again ripping open a deep gash in his neck as blood sprayed into the air and he fell over dead.

Shadow went into the home to find the little girl. He smelled her in a back bedroom, so he walked over to the big bed and looked under, and there she was, frightened and crying. She looked up and saw Shadow. She said, "Hello pretty kitty."

Shadow said, "Hello young lady. Now you will be safe." He heard a noise and turned just in time to see two orcs enter the room. They saw this large cat and slowly backed out. Shadow said, "Stay where you are. I'll be right back," and stood up and went through the door, saw the two orcs, and mumbled a simple spell. As the two orcs fell over dead, he came back and laid down by the bed and said, "Young lady, come out from under there, so I can take you somewhere safe."

She came out and climbed into his soft saddle.

They looked around and saw all the people slain along with some orcs and ogres. She found her family killed. She asked, "Can you please help me bury them?"

Shadow said, "Okay," and began to dig with his claws. Within minutes, he had three six-foot deep holes.

After the bodies were buried, she gave Shadow a hug then climbed back on. Shadow teleported them both back on top of the cliff. Shadow told her, "Here we go," as he began to run.

They came upon a crevice that Shadow leaped over once before. He told her to hang on as he jumped into the air and landed on the other side with ease. As he landed, she let out a giggle and said, "That was fun!"

He said, "Young lady, I have a very big surprise for you soon. But in the meantime, hold on to this teddy bear…" and one appeared in her arms.

She said, "Oh, thank you, pretty kitty," as he took off running again.

Soon they came to another wall, and Shadow started to climb up to a ledge. On that ledge was the opening to a dark cave. Shadow followed the tunnel back to the large cavern filled with treasure. Her first words were, "It's so dark in here."

Shadow cast a bright light spell and said, "All that you see is yours."

He let her climb down from his saddle, and she started to examine her new home.

About the same time, back at the castle, the ghost of the little girl holding the puppy told Mary, "Your gonna like this place, it's really neat." She vanished as she turned away.

Grunch told Mary, "I want to introduce you to Night Crawler. She is a good friend of mine."

They both vanished and reappeared in front of a very large wooden door. Grunch warned her about Night Crawler's children. Grunch slowly opened the door of a very dark room. The doors behind them slowly closed shut.

Mary told Grunch, "I can't see. It's total darkness."

Grunch cast a spell, as a ball of light appeared so she can see around her. There were sounds coming from every direction. Without warning, a small female spider two-feet around jumped up and wrapped her eight legs around Grunch, giving him another big hug as she said, "Welcome back, Uncle Grunch, we missed you!"

"This is Mary. I wanted to show her to you and let you know she is not to be harmed."

The small spider jumped from Grunch to Mary and gave her a hug, saying, "You're welcome here any time."

Mary couldn't speak; she just let out a gasp as the small spider jumped off and ran off into the darkness. Grunch said, "That's one of Night Crawler's children, come and meet their mother."

They walked deeper into the chamber until they came across a seven-foot-tall spider who was sleeping.

Grunch said, "Wakey, wakey, Night Crawler, I have someone here for you to meet."

Night crawler woke up and said, "Thank you for bringing me a meal…"

Grunch said, "NO! This is Mary, she will be living here, and she's not to be harmed."

Mary still could not speak; she'd never before seen a seven-foot-tall, talking spider. Night Crawler said, "I'm sorry for frightening you. It's nice to meet you. You're welcome anytime, my children and I will not hurt you."

Grunch asked, "Are you and your children hungry?" He snapped his fingers, and livestock appeared as they both vanished.

They both reappeared back in his room. Gunch asked, "Where's Shadow? We have unfinished business to attend to."

Mary asked, "What other creatures live in this castle with you?"

The phoenix sitting on his perch said, "You big bully, why didn't you tell her about the dragons?"

At that time, Zanlue entered the room to tell Grunch that Shadow was gone, and nobody knew where he went. Grunch told Mary, "Come with me. We're going to set Fluffy free."

Mary asked, "Who's Fluffy?"

Grunch called, "Here boy!" and a six-foot-tall, three-headed devil dog came running around a corner. Grunch said, "Don't worry; you'll be fine together." They walked to a hidden door. Grunch opened it to see the great outdoors with huge mountains. It was another realm for Fluffy to explore as Grunch turned to Mary and said, "He can live there forever." Then he closed the door.

They continued to walk down the hallway until they reached a wooden door at the end. They entered the room and found themselves on a large ledge of a cliff. They heard a very deep rumble and a loud voice that said, "It's about time you showed up, Grunch," as a huge, gold dragon appeared on the ledge. This female dragon stood 155 feet tall and 200 feet long. Her wing span was 200 feet. The gold dragon asked, "Who are you, young lady?"

Mary said, "M-m-m-my n-n-name is M-M-Mary, who are you?"

The dragon replied, "I am Moonlight, M-M-Mary. You can come back and visit me anytime."

Grunch said, "It's time to go," as a ring appeared on Mary's finger and she said, "Thank you." They vanished and reappeared on the beach to watch the sunset.

When the little girl got a better look at Shadow's fur and saw that it wasn't black at all (it was dark blue), she just said, "You are so pretty."

Shadow said, "You need clothes," as a pile appeared in all her favorite colors.

Mary said, "Thank you," as she gave him a big hug.

Shadow told her, "You will never be alone, and you will always be safe. I will always be near. Come with me now, I have a friend that you need to meet." And they both vanished and reappeared on the beach in front of Grunch's castle.

"It's about time you showed up. Who's that with you?"

Shadow filled Grunch in about the massacre of her village and the armies he saw building up. He told Grunch that he'd be taking care of her, so he would be staying with her for a little while.

Mary asked, "Can we go and visit the city?"

Shadow asked Mary and Mayflower if they would like to come along.

Mary said, "I have so much to do, but you go, Mayflower, and enjoy yourself."

Mayflower and Mars both climbed into Shadow's saddle, and the three vanished. They reappeared about a mile from the city.

As Shadow was walking with Mayflower and Mars on his back going to the city, some knights rode up from behind them, yelling, "Clear the road!"

Shadow stepped to the side, and all three saw the queen approach. Once she passed by, then they continued on their way. They entered the city by the market. People were staring. It was not every day a six-foot cat with two riders passed by.

Two knights approached and asked, "What's your business here?"

"We're looking for a nice place to have a meal, then buy some gifts."

One of the knights said, "You'll want John's shop. There's a diner next door that serves good meals, and they accept pets."

As they walked away, Shadow said, "Pets…? I'll show him a pet!" He mumbled something, and the knight's horse threw its rider, landing him in a mud puddle. Many people laughed at the knight's misfortune as Shadow walked on.

Mayflower said, "Look over there, those wizards are performing tricks for the children. Should we go show them a thing or two?"

Shadow trotted over to them and stopped. Mayflower told Mars to stay seated as she jumped down. When the wizards completed their tricks, Mayflower asked, "Can I try?"

One wizard said, "Little fairy, what can you do?"

Mayflower didn't hesitate, she mumbled some words that turned him from flesh to stone. She then asked the other wizards, "Any more questions?" She returned the wizard back to flesh and received a round of applause from the growing crowd. This wizard was speechless, not knowing what to say. His friend told him to leave them alone—"They have real magic."

Mayflower climbed back into the saddle, and Shadow found his way to the diner. As they were enjoying their meal, another wizard approached their table and said, "Shadow, is that you?"

Shadow stopped licking up his milk and said, "Well, hello Tom, my old friend! What brings you here?"

Tom said, "There's going to be a war coming soon to the north—ogres, orcs, hobgoblins, and giants are gathering together. To the east, the elves and dwarfs are putting their differences aside and are working together. In the west are zombies, ghouls, mummies, and werewolves that are joining forces. Humans gather to the south… I wouldn't want to be anywhere near when they meet. It's going to be quite a blood bath."

Mayflower asked, "How do you know all this?"

The wizard said, "I've witnessed the creatures to the north, and I've been given the gift of foresight. I have a favor to ask you? Can you please take this scroll to the city of Hope and give it to the monk at the monastery, so they, too, can be included in this war? I must go now. Thank you, my old friend. Remember that time is precious."

Shadow went back to his meal.

Mars said, "Oh goody, we get to go on an adventure!"

Mayflower said, "I'm going to pick up a gift, I'll see you back at Grunch's castle."

Mayflower went next door to the antique shop and was met by a small, gold dragon taking inventory. The dragon asked, "May I help you, young lady?"

She told him she needed a nice gift for a friend, and so the dragon was happy to help her. He picked out a nice crystal figurine as well as a practical gift of fur blankets. She said, "These will do nicely. Can you please gift wrap them for me?" As he was doing that, he could see that something was bothering her and asked what was wrong.

Mayflower said, "I have no way to bring these lovely gifts home. It's too far for my power to take me."

He asked, "Where do you need to go?" When she said the castle of Grunch, the dragon perked up and said, "I know of his place! I can send you there." The dragon mumbled a few words, and Mayflower vanished with her packages. she reappeared on the beach in front of Grunch's castle.

Shadow ran across a monk on the road, and asked, "Pardon me, sir, could you tell me how to get to the monastery in Hope?"

The monk said in surprise, "Hope? That's where I come from. I am on my way back home. Shadow offered to travel together back to the monastery and said, "This is my charge, Mars, she stays with me."

When they arrived at the monastery there were several monks training for battle.

Shadow asked, "Where can I find the head monk?"

The monk said, "The grand master will be training under the waterfall."

Mars asked, "Where is that?"

The monk said, "Follow the river until it falls over a cliff."

Shadow found the cliff. A hundred feet below, a monk sat on top of a boulder. Shadow jumped down with a splash, then walked over to the grand master and said, "I have a scroll for you."

He read it and said, "Very well, thank you." He scratched Shadow behind the ear and asked, "Can you two stay?"

Shadow replied, "Only for a short time."

"Good, come and join me for a meal."

Mars asked, "What kind of food do you eat here?"

"Tasty food. I think you'll like it."

When they arrived at the dining hall, every monk stood up in a show of respect until the grand master was seated. He waved his arms, and the tables were filled with food. The meal was better than Mars could ever hope for. She ate so much, her belly ached.

The grand master spoke up, addressing all of the monks. He said, "I have news to share with you all…" He read the scroll out loud and said, "Our time has come to join forces with the humans."

One monk questioned, "What have the humans done for us? Why should we join with them?"

The grand master said, "You are correct. The humans have done nothing for us, but this is who we are, and we cannot turn away."

Shadow said, "We thank you for your hospitality, but now we really must go. But before we go, I must say that humans are dumb, ignorant, and selfish; but it's time to put all differences aside and help each other for the greater good. A war is brewing, and even the gods will be fighting."

He then looked at Mars and they both vanished, they reappeared at the front door to Grunch's castle. Shadow said, "Look at all the beautiful flowers, aren't they pretty? Grunch doesn't even know that these flowers exist. Shall we go inside? I'll show you around a little."

As the sun began to set, they went inside to let Grunch know of the upcoming war.

Grunch said that he already knew it was going to happen, but he didn't know when. After a fine meal and a night of relaxation, Grunch told Shadow and Mayflower that his time was growing short, and there was some business he had to tend to.

And with that, he vanished.

4

THE GODDESS OF RAMPAGE

Grunch reappeared at the cave of John and Tina. He wanted to speak with Tina. He wanted to honor her with a gift but needed to know if it was something she'd be interested in. He sat on a boulder to think about what was about to happen while waiting for Tina to emerge from the cave home.

When she arrived, he said, "I have a surprise for you, Tina." He snapped his fingers, and they were transported to another world filled with pure beauty. He said, "As you know, I have great power, but my time grows short. Would you be willing to take my place as the goddess of rampage?"

"Are you sure you want me?"

Grunch said, "Yes, but you'll need to grow much stronger for the job."

She said, "I would be honored to do as you ask."

He opened his hand, and a small knife appeared. He reached for her hand and cut slices from their palms. He gripped her hand tight, so their blood would mix. When this was done, he said, "Next step, we must take a trip to mountain Olympus and petition the gods. Only with their approval, may you become a goddess." He snapped his fingers, and they both appeared on a platform in front of Zeus and other gods.

As Grunch spoke to the gods letting them know of his desire, she remained silently standing by his side. Approval was given by Zeus. Zeus said, "Listen to Grunch. He will teach you well. He has trained many of us here."

Grunch and Zeus shook hands, and then Grunch and Tina vanished, only to reappear back at the entrance to Tina and John's cave. Grunch said,

"Rest well. Your training will begin at first light. You will learn combat, spells, and languages."

The next morning, Grunch took them both to a run-down shack in the middle of the woods. He told her to wait by a stump while he went inside. A short time later, he came out with a friend. Tina was surprised to see Grunch with a half-giant. He told her, "This is Brock, and he will teach you how to fight." Grunch took a seat on the stump and simply said, "Brock will try to hurt you now."

She said, "But, but—he's huge! You can't be serious."

Grunch said, "Protect yourself," as Brock walked over and swiftly kicked Tina in the chest, sending her flying backwards. She landed on her butt and quickly got up, saying, "Let's fight!" as they both rushed in, colliding with great force and knocking each other off their feet. After the first hour, she felt beaten up with cuts and bruises all over, but she wasn't about to give up. She punched Brock in the chest, sending him flying back 10 feet. Tina was surprised by this new ability and was more determined than ever to win this fight.

Before Brock could get up, Tina was standing on his chest. As she looked at her wounds and saw them heal before her eyes, Brock said, "Good fight."

Grunch said, "Very well. This lesson is complete. Shall we have lunch?"

After their meal, Grunch thanked Brock and told Tina, "We have more work to do. They vanished, only to reappear back in his castle in a spell room with a golden dragon reading a spell book. Grunch said, "You will read each of these books."

She thought, *There's just no way...*

Grunch said, "Quit thinking, and just do it," as he left.

The dragon said, "I take care of this place, so anything you need, I will be glad to help you find it." He handed Tina a book, and before she could open it, she had the whole thing memorized. It seemed she could absorb the knowledge of the book simply by holding it. By supper time, she had the whole library read. She looked forward to a break and enjoyed her meal.

Later, she was taken to another library and was told, "These are all the languages of all the lands. There are scrolls with more spells to learn. This will take you most of the night. Make sure to get some rest. Tomorrow is going to be another busy day."

Day after day went by, and Tina learned so much about her new abilities. She could do things she could only dream of! She thought, *Won't John be surprised when he sees me again!*

Near the end of the month, Grunch let her know that he would be testing her on everything she learned. When the day came for her test, Grunch took her to another large cave. He said, "Today will be my last day, but the beginning of a whole new life for you. Prepare to defend yourself."

As he crossed the room, he fired four magic missiles at her. She easily stepped to the side as they struck the wall behind her. She sent two huge fireballs back at him, but Grunch just batted them away only to find two ice missiles behind them as he was hit in the chest and stumbled backwards. He thought, *That's a good move.*

He cast a 10-foot ring of fire around her, and she levitated a large rock and threw it at him. With a wave of his hand, the rock exploded. He slashed the air with his open hand, and a gash opened up on her arm. She laughed and said, "I can do much better!" She said a few quiet words and Grunch's arm swelled up until to exploded!

He said, "It's about to get bloody. Now let's see what you can do!" He waved his good arm, and half of her face sprayed blood out in all directions. She moaned in pain and he said, "Give me your best shot."

She said, "How can I fight like this?"

But as she said the words, her vision returned to normal, and her wounds were beginning to heal. She had an evil grin on her face when she conjured hands of stone from the ground to hold him in place. While he was trying to free himself, she cast a no-resistance spell.

He said, "Nice try, but that won't work on either of us."

He freed himself from the stone hands and sent over a dozen flaming arrows. She waved her hand, and they simply vanished. She took a step back and summoned all her strength and cast a very powerful spell of disintegration, hitting Grunch square in the chest.

She cried, "Oh my god, what have I done!"

Grunch smiled, and his last words were: "Well done. You pass..." as he disappeared.

Tina stood alone in the cave. A flash of light appeared, and Zeus was standing in front of her. He said, "You've passed the final test. Welcome Tina, goddess of rampage. Use your gifts well." Then he vanished, leaving her alone again.

She had much to do and no time to mourn the loss of her friend; that time would come later. She thought about home, and she appeared at the mouth of her cave. She missed John and her daughters and was happy to see them, but she wasn't sure how to tell them that she was now a goddess. She went inside and found her family over whelmed with joy. She said, "I have a surprise for you all. While I've been gone, I've been working on myself." She snapped her fingers, and the dining chamber was filled with exotic foods.

John said, "I've only seen Grunch do that. How is this possible?"

Tina told him, "Grunch is no more. I am the new goddess of rampage."

John didn't believe her until they went into town and where Grunch's statue was, and now, there stood a beautiful statue of his wife. Many people were praying for her. He said, "I need a drink," and took Tina to the tavern. He ordered a pitcher of beer, and she paid with gold coins.

While at the tavern, six big men came up to them. The biggest man pushed John, trying to start a fight. Tina said, "Don't worry, I can take care of this." She grabbed the man by his neck and picked him up, slamming him through a table. The rest of them backed away. She said, "John, I think it's time to go."

John asked, "Really? Who are you?"

She said, "I thought you'd like being married to a goddess."

John said, "You can show me what more you can do."

Tina snapped her fingers, and they reappeared back in their cave. Tina heard a voice in her mind saying, *Help me please!* It sounded frightened. She told John she had business to take care of and vanished, reappearing at the edge of a swamp. Above was a cage hanging from the tree tops. Inside the cage was a seven-year-old girl. On the shore, dressed in all black was a human man. Before she could do anything, he changed into a medium black dragon.

She said, "I'll give you one chance. Free the girl, and I'll let you live."

He laughed and sprayed fire on her. It had no effect on Tina. She quickly said a flesh to stone spell and turned the dragon into a statue. She then freed the girl and sent her on her way home.

Tina returned back to John. He said, I hope it was nothing important, you weren't gone very long."

"It wasn't anything."

"I guess I'll have to get used to things like that from now on."

As Tina was talking to John, they heard a man's voice saying, "Please help me," and he told Tina of a giant terrorizing the country side. She told him not to worry; she'd take care of it. "Duty calls," she said to John, and she vanished with her visitor to reappear back at his farm. There, she found a broken fence along with some missing horses. She sat on the porch to wait for the giant's return. While waiting, she enjoyed a cup of milk and some cookies.

Shortly, a 30-foot tall forest giant walked across the field to the remaining horses. Tina stood up and started walking up towards him as a beautiful longsword appeared in her hands. The giants' eyes grew wide as she swung the sword, slicing a very deep gash across his leg.

As he growled in pain, he fell to the ground on one knee. She again attacked burying the sword all the way to the hilt in his chest, killing the giant as blood poured out. She didn't know it, but the killing was witnessed by Zeus.

She returned to John to make plans to move into the castle. It took them only a day for the move. Tina's new powers made things easy. While settling in at the castle, the phoenix was there on his perch and spoke up, saying, "You can't tell me what to do, you dumb girl."

Tina went to the bird and grabbed it by the neck, saying, "You will NOT talk to me like that! This is my new home!" As she let lose, she turned and ran into Shadow so hard that she fell backwards. When she picked herself up, she asked, "May I ask you a question? Why did you sneak up on me like that?"

"I'm a cat. That's what I do."

It took her almost a full month to get to know her new home. It was full of surprises. As she sat there, she thought to herself that she couldn't be as cruel as Grunch. She could sense that there was trouble near. She blinked and appeared in the forbidden forest, staring into the eyes of an orcki. She asked, "What are you doing here?"

He said, "We hunt orcs."

She said, "I've got a deal for you, Grinlore. If you keep patrol of this area, I will give you armor and better weapons, and you are always welcome at my castle."

He said, "Thank you, but we must know: Who are you?"

She said, "My name is Tina, I am the goddess of rampage." As she began to vanish, she said, "If you need me, just call for me."

She returned back to John. John said, "I don't know if I can handle you going into danger so often."

Her reply was not what John had expected. She pulled out a hatchet and cut off her little finger.

Within seconds, she started to regenerate and said, "See John? I feel it, but it grows back. It makes it hard to hurt me. If you would like to take the girls and go visit your mother, I understand. This is my life now; you must accept me for who I am. Come back to me after you feel better about my life." The girls arrived, and she teleported the three of them to his mothers.

After a few minutes, she got a tingling feeling throughout her body. As Normax the wizard appeared in front of her with his eyes glowing light blue, he asked, "Where is Mayflower?"

She answered, "Why are you in my home?"

He said, "I am here to teach Mayflower the art of sorcery."

He found Mayflower sitting in a beautiful garden. As it was getting dark, she said, "Look at the bright star in the sky." She snapped her fingers, and it vanished. She laughed as it came back a few minutes later.

Normax said, "Very impressive. You have learned a lot; not like that idiot dragon Zanlue. I'm surprised he hasn't blown himself up yet."

"There have been a few explosions in the middle of the night," she replied.

The phoenix was sitting on his perch and said, "You lazy girl, you could have been done hours ago!" Mayflower grabbed him by the neck and started shaking the bird.

The next morning, Tina called Kindle and Dwindle to her throne room. She said that there were forces gathering for a great battle; "I'm sending both of you to the south." She snapped her fingers, and they were dressed in black armor with battle war hammers at their sides. She said, "Be careful," as she waved her hand and the twins were gone.

They reappeared on the shore across from the island. They started traveling, and a short time later, they heard sounds off in the distance. They went and found an old man trying to pull a cart. Kindle asked, "May we help you?"

He said, "Thank you." They pulled his cart all the way into town. They decided to go to the local tavern. He said, "I'm in your debt," when all three entered the tavern.

It was the largest tavern that the twins had ever seen. It had three levels with balconies. They found a corner table and sat down. Without warning, a human body crashed through their table. Kindle jumped to his feet as a large man came near. Kindle punched the man, sending him backward into a group of dwarf berserkers still wearing their bloody spike battle gear. This was the beginning of an all-out brawl. Within minutes, the floor was littered with blood and humans. The berserkers sat back down and started drinking and laughing with their two new dwarfen friends.

During the evening, Kindle and Dwindle found out that they were all going the same way, and Kindle asked if they could join their little group. One of the berserkers said, "Yes. Now there are 10 of us, we can fight small groups of orcs that we had seen along the way."

In the morning, they all started out only to find themselves wandering through an old graveyard. Before long, five ghouls jumped out and started attacking them, but the berserkers were ready to fight. The attack wasn't long before the ghouls laid in heaps on the battleground. As they settled down for their noon meal, Dwindle said, "Me, me, brother, *oof!*" as they both laughed at the joke.

When Tina showed up, she asked, "Is this how you patrol the forest?" As she looked around at the motley group, she said, "I guess traveling together is a good idea." She raised her hand, and four ghouls dropped dead on the spot. She said, "There's a hut in the next valley, give this message to the woman living there." Then, she vanished.

They packed their gear and started to head out. A little way down the road, they heard a battle taking place. They found six knights fighting eight hill giants. The dwarfs joined the fight.

Without a sound, Dwindle ran up with his war hammer, smashing one of the hill giants in the knee. As he fell to the ground, he yelled in pain. When a knight took his longsword and ran his blade all the way through the hill giants' neck, spraying blood in all directions, one of the hill giants took his club and hit one of the knights so hard that his armor was crushed as he fell to the ground, dead.

A hill giant fell over a dead body, giving Kindle a chance to crush his head with his war hammer. Kindle swung with all his might, smashing the hill giants head sending blood and brain to run out onto the ground. In a short time, the giants lay dead, along with three other knights. The remaining knights gathered their dead, and one said to the dwarfs, "Thank you," as they parted ways. The dwarfs took a break and made camp for the night.

The next morning, when Kindle and Dwindle woke up, the other dwarfs were gone, so they started to travel through the valley of the undead souls. It wasn't long before they found the hut with a very beautiful lady. Kindle handed her the scroll and watched as she read the message and said, "It's from my sister. She would like me to join your group traveling south. I am a woman of very strong magic, and you two may need my help. We will leave after you two have a fine meal." The dwarfs ate their fill and sat back to rest before continuing their journey.

As the three started out again, they left the valley and traveled through another graveyard. They hoped this one would be peaceful, but they were wrong. Four undead spectra arose from their graves and started flying toward them. The woman said, "Stand behind me!" as she raised her hand. She summoned a powerful spell that made them vanish.

As they left the graveyard behind, they came to a fork in the road. One way circled back around to the graveyard, and the other went to the deep dark forest. The twins and the woman continued their journey until a man jumped out with a short sword in his hand. He demanded money. Before either of them could do anything, the lady said a few words, and the stranger fell to the ground and began to transform into stone.

As the group left him there and continued on their way, they reached the edge of the forest where thousands of humans were gathering for the battle to come. The three of them were taken to the men in charge and received several scrolls to take back to Tina. They stayed long enough to have a meal and then they left.

They reached a fork in the road by sunset and decided to make camp for the night. They got an early start and knew there was a graveyard to cross. They hoped it would be empty, but they weren't so lucky.

As a fog rolled in, a dragon lich emerged and attacked without warning. As a claw struck Kindle, tearing him in half. Dwindle ran to his brother's side. As the dragon, without a sound, bit down and removed his head as his body fell to the ground.

The lady was able use a very powerful spell, exploding the dragon into pieces. She was wondering how she would find her sister, and she whispered, "Tina, where are you?"

Just then, Tina appeared and said, "Penny, I heard you call my name," as they embraced each other.